Look for these titles from Cari Griffin

Now Available

Catering to Billionaires

Triple Layer Love

A Spirited Threesome

Too Hot to Handle

Finding Their Treasure

Serving All Three

Cookie Nookie

Wild Ride

Wild Magic: Fortune's Fancy

COOKIE NOOKIE

M/M/F Ménage Romance

CARI GRIFFIN

etopia
press

Etopia Press
1643 Warwick Ave., #124
Warwick, RI 02889
http://www.etopia-press.net

COOKIE NOOKIE

First Etopia Press electronic publication: September 2019

First Etopia Press print publication: March 2020

~ DEDICATION ~

To Mary L.

CHAPTER ONE

Rebecca

Rebecca Johnson finished arranging her free cookie samples on the table at her booth. She placed the plastic sneeze covers over each serving dish. With that done, she walked out to the aisle, put her hands on her hips, and gave her booth a last once-over before the Bakers of New England tradeshow opened.

Everything had to be perfect. The cookies. The big banner sign for Cookie Nookie, her little shop on the main street of Freemont. Her special paper plates with her shop's name and logo on them. She'd wanted the napkins to have her logo too, but she'd been at the end of her advertising budget. So sacrifices had to be made.

On top of all that, she had spent a lot of money renting even a small space here at the civic center for this trade show. It would be worth it if she could snag a couple more restaurants or small shops that would use her "taste of homemade" cookies in their desserts or re-sell them to the tourist trade.

Around her, the low murmur of conversation filled the air from organizers, attendants, and other booth owners racing to set up before the show opened in half an hour. She pulled out her cell phone and glanced at the time again. Exactly five minutes had passed since she'd checked five minutes ago.

All in all, her vendor booth looked pretty good, given her tight budget. She had three folding tables with special tablecloths with the Cookie Nookie logo emblazoned on the sides. Her banner might be the same one she'd used at last year's show, but it was still plenty razzy and snazzy.

Rebecca had samples of a wide variety of her cookies on the main table. Chocolate chip, oatmeal with or without raisins, molasses, butterscotch, gingersnaps, peanut butter, shortbread, snickerdoodle (too fun to say), sugar cookies, New York-style black-and-white cookies, and all kinds of macaroons. She had everything from rolled, drop, fried, pressed, molded, and sandwich cookies. If it was a cookie, she could bake it.

She had boxes of cookies on the table to her right, ready to be sold to anyone tempted by one of her heavenly sinful samples. The table on her right had information on her cookie ingredients (*only the best!*), her store location (*right downtown, a charming little nook you can't miss!*), buying-in-bulk options (*the more, the merrier! Parties welcome!*), and touting her online store. Want some more delicious and unforgettable Cookie Nookie cookies but don't live in Maine? Order online and have them shipped straight to your door!

So far, her online cookie sales had been struggling to gain steam. The pedestrian traffic into her little cookie shop wedged between a huge bank and the gigantic post office building was descent, although highly dependent on tourist traffic. Tourism had seen a slump in the area this year. What she really depended on was the steady supply of business from restaurants, tourist shops, and even local grocery stores that bought and resold her cookies.

But now, all of that was in danger thanks to one thing. Lighthouse Bakery Company.

Don't look at them, she warned herself. *Don't even turn around and look. You'll never be able to keep the vengeful fire out of your eyes.*

That was good advice. She would stand here admiring her own booth, and she *wouldn't* turn around to glare at the huge, dominate-the-whole-civic-center "booth" run by Lighthouse Bakery Company. After all, what good would that do?

She turned around and glared anyway. She couldn't help it. She was only human.

The Lighthouse Bakery Company had just come to Portland, Maine. They'd broken ground six months ago and just finished building a large industrial bakery scheduled to open next month. Yes, she was very nervous about it. Even though her little shop was in a different town south of Portland, Lighthouse was already spreading its evil influence in all directions, all while lauding itself as "returning good jobs to Maine." As if the world needed more mass-produced cookies instead of handcrafted, lovingly made cookies, which were as American as apple pie and jazz.

Her eyes narrowed as she looked over Lighthouse's elaborate vendor area right across the aisle from her. Her booth was up against the wall, but Lighthouse had prime floor space, dominating the area. She shouldn't be jealous, but of course, she was.

Everything about the Lighthouse booth screamed "well-funded." Fancy, high-def TV monitors showing footage of the equipment or highly produced shots of their products—bread, pastries, and cookies of course. There were illuminated signs. Slick, well-dressed attendants. Lots of hugely blown-up photos of their baked goods, professionally done and must have cost an arm and a leg. They also had plenty of samples...and plenty of employees to help set everything up.

As she looked over the Lighthouse area with scorn (and envy), her gaze suddenly landed on two men talking on the far side. All her competitive ire drained out of her. She stopped glaring and bit the inside of her cheek instead. She had to. Because otherwise she'd be licking her lips. And that would mess up her lipstick.

The strength of her reaction surprised and annoyed her. This wasn't the time for man ogling, no matter how good they looked.

And they looked good.

Both men were unfairly handsome. It wasn't right for men to look that way. All broad shoulders and chiseled jaws and that man way of standing as if they were dominating the space they were in.

It was distracting and wrong.

They were both strangers to her, but judging from where they were standing, they clearly had some connection to Lighthouse. They were deep in some kind of discussion—probably how to better use their axis of bakery evil against small-town America—but the man closest to her was grinning. He had a beautiful smile. A toothpaste-commercial-level smile. The man was wearing a perfectly tailored business suit that reeked of money even from this far away. He was tall, deliciously fit and handsome enough to be on television. He had dirty blonde hair that came down to his shoulders, a bit tousled-looking, the kind of hair you wanted to run your hands through. Or hair you could grip when he went down between your legs...

Ahem. None of that. She was here for business. Her shop might be called Cookie Nookie, but that was only because her shop was wedged into a nook, and her other two name choices had already been trademarked. At the time, she'd thought it was clever and memorable. But having to explain it to people had long grown tiresome, but Cookie Love didn't have the same ring to it.

Anyway, the guy she was drooling over filled out his suit wonderfully, with broad shoulders and, honestly, a nice butt.

The second guy was just as gorgeous but in a different way. He had brown hair, cut short enough to be bristly. He wore a button-up, blue-gray work shirt with long sleeves, jeans, and boots. He was watching the suit guy with the attention and focus of an employee taking orders. He also had a jaw so chiseled he could use it to break down doors, an impressive set of pecs bulging out that work shirt in all the right ways.

She couldn't see his butt from the way he was standing, but given that chest and flat stomach, she was willing to bet it was tight enough to bounce quarters off of. But why throw quarters at a good ass? She'd rather squeeze it and—

Whoa. Whoa. Whoa. Her libido was out of control. Yeah, it had been months (okay, a year at least) since she'd gotten good and laid. Since her last relationship had fizzled out, in fact. But that didn't mean she could excuse drooling over the enemy. Those two men were in the Lighthouse Bakery vendor area, and that made them the enemy.

Rebecca nodded to herself and walked back behind her tables to put some distance between them. Besides, her traitor body needed to be reined in before her panties got soaked. She had a job to do here. She didn't have the luxury of ogling man-candy. She didn't know who the second guy was—maybe an attendant there for moving tables and equipment—but the guy in the suit had to be the infamous Jack Meacham, the billionaire behind Lighthouse Bakery.

She didn't pay much attention to the news because it was always bad, but she'd seen a story in the paper that Jack Meacham was some big investor who'd been born in Maine and made his fortune in New York. Now he wanted to return and start a bunch of business ventures in Maine. She didn't know why. Maybe he felt guilty for leaving. Maybe he'd been banned from New York. Maybe he was obsessed with lobsters.

Rebecca didn't know; she didn't care.

She needed to focus on herself and her mission right now. And that mission was enticing restaurants or small shops to buy her homemade-style cookies. At the trade show last year, she'd picked up three new clients, two of which were still with her.

Speaking of which, how much longer until this show started? She checked the time, saw they had another fifteen minutes until the doors opened to the public. She was eager for it to start, but also nervous as hell that things wouldn't go well. That Lighthouse would suck all the oxygen out of the civic center.

After a furtive glance around, she used her cell phone's selfie camera setting to check her hair and makeup. Yes, it was silly. She'd put her face on (as her mother liked to say) at five in the morning because she couldn't sleep. But she wanted to check and make sure she hadn't messed up her lipstick while drooling over those two guys.

Thankfully, her lipstick was fine. She looked okay enough. She'd gone with baker's whites and an apron. Wearing other professional clothes wouldn't give the same homemade air she relied on.

She snorted. Maybe she should've dusted herself with flour too. Gone for the gold when it came to baker clichés.

Rebecca turned off the phone's camera, frowning, tired of looking at herself. She'd never been able to escape the "cute" look. Not beautiful, glamorous, stunning, or anything close to a runway model. Cute. Like a panda bear. It didn't help that she had never been able to fit into size negative dresses either. Her mother had always made sure to call her fat, but her mother could be a bitch with an acid tongue. Sure, she was a little thick in places. Quite a few places. But she still had an hourglass figure. Just a thick one. With big boobs. And a big butt. And maybe her face was a little round. Round but cute.

Take that, Mom.

She pushed those memories of her mother out of

her mind. They did no one any good. Rebecca was a successful—mildly so—businesswoman. She didn't have time for that emotional crap.

She ate a cookie. Just because she could.

She closed her eyes, reveling in the taste. For the love of all that was holy, did it ever taste good.

"Excuse me," a woman's sharp voice said, interrupting her cookie nirvana. "Are you Rebecca Johnson?"

She swallowed her half-chewed mouthful and tried not to wipe her lips with the back of her hand. Smeared lipstick would do none of them any favors.

"Yes," she finally managed. "I'm Rebecca."

"I need you to move your booth fifty feet that way," the woman, who looked like an evil librarian, said as she pointed farther down the civic center. "You are in reserved space."

"What? One of the organizers *specifically* told me this was my spot." She tried to keep her voice steady, but some outrage managed to creep in anyway. She had just finished setting up. It had taken forever to get everything even close to perfect.

"Whoever told you that was mistaken." The

woman brandished a paper at her, stabbing it with a bony finger. "See? You're here. This entire area was reserved by someone else."

Rebecca's eyes widened as she noticed who the area was reserved for. Lighthouse Bakery Company.

Those bastards! Even now, they worked to destroy her.

"Look," she said, giving her most charming smile and really turning it on. "I'm not bothering anyone here. I'm not even in their way." She waved a hand at the sprawling Lighthouse vendor section. "They're clearly already set up. Can I just stay here for today?"

She tried to look cute and non-troublesome, eager to please but hoping for someone to (please just once in her life) throw her a bone.

It didn't work.

"I'm sorry. The floor plan can't be changed. You're going to have to move all of—" She waved a hand at Rebecca's tables and boxes and brochures. "*This*." She eyed the banner sign. "And I'm not sure who approved your company's name. It's not very family-friendly."

"Listen," she said, feeling a bit desperate. "It's not like that. My store is this little place, like a nook. Like...an alcove. Between a bank and the post office. So...nook rhymes with cook, and nookie rhymes with cookie..."

The woman was staring at her as if she'd grown two heads and six horns. She marked something down on her digital computer pad, scowling as if Rebecca should be stoned to death for the name of her shop. A name that maybe had a little double entendre, but hell, it was all in fun.

"Just make sure you move your booth," the woman said coldly. "I'll be back in fifteen minutes to check."

Damn you, Lighthouse Bakery. She wanted to march over there and tell them off for being such heartless, coldblooded lizards who didn't know a thing about real baking. Baking with heart.

But of course she didn't. She didn't make a scene. She only nodded until the woman zoomed off to sting someone else. Sighing, Rebecca turned back to her little booth with all the carefully arranged everything.

She was going to have to start from scratch. And

she had about ten minutes to get this done before the doors opened to the public.

What was it they said online these days? FML?

Yes, *fuck my life* indeed.

"I couldn't help but notice that Sandy descended on you like a praying mantis," a smooth male baritone said from behind her.

Rebecca jumped. People kept sneaking up and ambushing her today, and that didn't make any sense because this was a civic center and not some shadowy alleyway.

She whirled around. And found herself face to face with Mr. Gorgeous Blond Guy in the Designer Suit. The guy from the Lighthouse booth.

That she *hadn't* been drooling over earlier.

"I'm sorry," he said, but his smile said he was mildly sorry at best. Sorry, but more amused than anything. "I didn't mean to startle you."

"You didn't," she lied. "I was focused on..."

Why on Earth was she talking to this guy? He was the enemy. He might look like some kind of California lifeguard packed into an expensive suit, but he was the epitome of evil corporate greed.

He lifted his eyebrows, waiting for her to finish. Those brows were thick. Not unibrow-level thick, but manly. Virile.

Holy Mother of Vanilla Extract, had she just called a man's eyebrows virile? She needed to go find a dark corner and lie down for a while. Clearly, she had heatstroke or something.

"They told me I need to move," she finally said. "She said I'm in…someone else's space." She wasn't going to say the name Lighthouse Bakery out loud. "But an hour ago, another organizer or floor manager or whatever told me to set up right here."

He tilted his head a little and rubbed his chin. He was perfectly clean-shaven, but she guessed he looked just as handsome with some shadow of facial hair. Men had it so easy. She wished she could get away with growing hair on her face—wait, no, she took that back. She really didn't want that.

He jerked a thumb toward the Lighthouse area behind him. "I can go talk to the big cheese over there and see if he'll let you stay where you are. I don't think they're going to use it. You know corporate guys. Buying up all the space they can whether they need it or not."

She eyed him distrustfully. "Aren't you...with them?" She looked him over again. The suit was definitely tailored, probably something Italian. The shoes, also expensive Italian. But now that he was this close and from this angle, she could see he was wearing a...a Hawaiian print tie. And a pocket square to match. It was colorful. It was bold. And it wasn't what she expected.

He grinned and shrugged. "I know a few people over there. One of them is my boyfriend." He paused, thinking about it. "It always sounds strange calling a guy over thirty a 'boyfriend.'"

"You're not...Jack Meacham?"

"Nope. And I don't know anything about baking or the food industry." He eyed her display of cookies. "Except I'm an expert in knowing what I like. May I?"

"Go ahead," she said, a little stunned. So he was gay. Wasn't that just her luck? She had the attention of a gorgeous hunk who was obviously rich as sin (not that that mattered, but it was a nice perk, wasn't it?) and the guy liked other dudes.

He used tongs to take a cookie from her sample

plate and then replaced the clear plastic cover. He took a big bite while she watched his mouth and wondered why he had such great lips. Genetic engineering?

Geez, what was wrong with her brain today? Guys who looked like this weren't interested in girls like her. The "cute-at-best" ones with a little too much packed onto the caboose. They dated aspiring actresses and pantyhose models.

He moaned, his eyes widening as he chewed the cookie. The sound...well, it did things to her. Spawned naughty thoughts. Made her imagine things she would need her vibrator to help with later tonight.

"Pardon my French," he said, staring at the cookie in his hand, one big chunk now missing. "But this is a damn good cookie."

She flushed with pleasure. She was a sucker for people who complimented her baking. And from that decadent moan, he hadn't been acting. "Thank you."

He took another bite, clearly enjoying it. "So, for this piece of cookie heaven, I'd gladly go over and see if they'll let you keep your booth here."

"No, thank you. I don't want any problems." She shook her head. "Not with Lighthouse or with the civic center. I'll just move. I don't want them doing me any special favors."

She had enough problems with Lighthouse as it was. Namely, them charging in and taking over all the business in the area. And they probably didn't even know her shop existed.

The man watched her, a slight frown on his face but sympathy in his eyes. He seemed to be one of those very warm, very charming people. She guessed he never had a problem keeping his bed full of willing partners.

Finally, he nodded. He chowed down on the rest of the cookie, licked his fingers, and laughed. "I suppose that's not very good manners, but that was good."

She handed him a napkin, smiling. She didn't have to worry that he was lying to her for ulterior motives, especially since both of them liked men...which put them on the same team, she guessed. "Thank you. It's always something special when someone enjoys something I've made."

He nodded. "All right. Now down to business. Since you don't want me to use my incredible powers

of persuasion to let you stay here in enemy territory..."
He cracked his knuckles and sized up her booth. "Let's
get you moved."

"Oh! You don't have to! I can do it." And had he
just called Lighthouse *enemy territory*? Was he a mind
reader?

He was smirking at her. His eyes were hazel
with a burst of color ringing the iris. Almost amber.
She'd never quite seen anything like them.

"I *do* have to. You bought my services with a
cookie."

That made her laugh. "Those are free samples."

"You can't put a price on a good cookie. Well, I
suppose you can. But what I mean is, if you would like
help, then I would love to lift and carry. As a male, it is
my primary reason for being on this planet."

"Well... Okay." She glanced at one of the wall
clocks. The show would open to the public any minute.
She really didn't have time to make a show of standing
on pride right now. She needed the help.

Working together, they managed to lift and
carry the three tables fifty feet down the side aisle
where the woman had ordered her to move. They did it

one at a time, and with his help, she didn't have to unload everything, pack it up, then unpack and set up again. Only a little straightening was necessary. Not one cookie box or napkin fell on the floor. And together, they took down and re-hung her banner sign too.

After it was done, the man made a show of wiping his brow. "That was exhausting. I think I might need another cookie to recharge my depleted energy stores."

She grinned and gave him a box. "Here. This is an assortment of our most popular cookies. You've certainly earned it." She paused, looking into his eyes, not sure what to do with all the gratitude that had her choked up. "And…thank you again for your help."

He held the box almost reverently, staring at it as if she'd given him something valuable instead of just a box of cookies. *Her* cookies, yes, and they were great, but they weren't exactly going to save the world through chocolate chips.

When he looked at her again, there was a twinkle in his eye. Her heart actually did a little stutter-stop. He really was handsome. When he turned on the charm, it was stunning. She didn't even know his name, and already she felt like she knew him. How weird was that?

"If you need anything else," he said with that warm-syrup smile, "just let me know. I come cheap. A box of cookies and I'm yours for life."

She laughed again. "I'm sure your boyfriend wouldn't like that."

Now his grin turned naughty. "Oh, don't worry. He likes to share." With that, he lifted the box to her in a goodbye salute and headed back toward the Lighthouse Bakery area.

"Wait!" she called, not sure why, but not quite willing to have him walk away. Not yet. To think she'd believed him that jerk Jack Meacham just because he liked expensive suits. "What's your name?"

"Liam Collins, at your service." He made a show of bowing, which actually had her giggling at the silliness of it all. It impressed her that Liam didn't seem to care if people thought him silly or strange. That confidence was refreshing. She wished she had more of it herself. "And your name?" he asked.

"Rebecca Johnson," she said, for some reason,

the back of her neck going hot.

"Well, Ms. Johnson, I love your cookies, and I love the name of your shop. It marries two of my favorite things." He grinned and winked at her—not something every man could pull off, but he did it easily.

She watched him walk back to the Lighthouse Bakery booth. Then she realized she was staring at his ass beneath the suit jacket. She blushed and looked away. She was clearly out of control.

But who could blame her? A guy looking like that? He was inviting a little ogling. A little private-fantasy indulgence—

Her thoughts broke off as the first members of the public began filing through the doors from the civic center's huge foyer.

Quickly, Rebecca rechecked everything for the tenth time and sat down in her chair, plastering a smile on her face.

She was ready to sell some cookies and entice some new patrons, winning some new businesses.

If she wanted her shop to stay open, she didn't have a choice.

* * *

Jack

"What are you up to?" Jack asked Liam when the man came wandering over again from the woman he'd been helping.

"I was aiding a damsel in distress," Liam said with a grin. "It's healthy for the ego. You know that."

Jack scowled and looked at the woman again. She was dressed in a baking outfit, complete with apron over a white, long-sleeved, double-breasted jacket, and topped off with a white chef's hat. She had brown hair beneath the hat, pulled back in a braid. The bright red and black logo on her signs said "Cookie Nookie" and "Home-style Cookies Made with Love."

He grunted. Last time he'd checked, love wasn't on the FDA-approved list of ingredients. She was cute enough, high cheekbones, big eyes, and—his gaze dropped lower—big breasts. No wonder Liam had wandered over to her. He loved big breasts. He was a male cliché like that.

"She doesn't look that distressed to me, Mr. White Knight," he said, eyeing Liam.

"Well, she's not actually. But she eventually accepted my help because I can be so charming." He shrugged and leaned against a table with his hands in his pockets. "Why are you in such a prickly mood?"

"I'm not." But he was, and he knew it. He wanted everything at the Lighthouse display to be perfect. Dealing with the usual run of problems had him in his focused work mode. That mode was curt and direct and didn't have time for a lot of nonsense.

Liam only gave him that grin that said Liam knew he was full of shit. He couldn't fool Liam. He never could.

And it didn't help that Liam looked so damn good that Jack wanted to drag him into a kiss right here and now. But that was out of the question. The public was filing through the doors and onto the civic center floor. This wasn't his New York City or Liam's L.A. This was Maine. Attitudes might be changing about men loving men, but that didn't mean sucking face in the middle of their booth before the Lighthouse Bakery

Company's grand opening was a good idea.

So he clamped down on the desire he could feel heating up inside him, looking at Liam with his perfectly disheveled hair, his Brioni suit, those amazingly soulful eyes that always managed to heat his blood to boiling, and feeling nothing but regret because this wasn't the time or the place.

In fact, it was annoying that the other man looked so damn good right now. Jack was wearing clothes he could work in—jeans and a work shirt. He had all the ten-thousand-dollar suits he could want, but when he was in the trenches like today, he dressed for getting his hands dirty.

But Liam was so laidback that he never cared much, one way or another. If he wanted to wear a suit, he wore a suit. If he wanted casual, he rocked that too. He went with the flow, let the good times roll.

Jack rolled his eyes. Californians. They were like an alien species.

"Why did you wear that suit here anyway?" he demanded, frowning at Liam as if the man had done it just to spite him. Which he might have...especially with that crazy Hawaiian tie and pocket square that were in such bad taste that they transcended and became stylish again.

Only Liam could pull something like that off.

"What can I say?" Liam's eyes twinkled. "I wanted to dress up."

"You wanted to annoy me."

Liam shrugged. "Maybe I wanted to impress you. Turn you on. Lure you into the restrooms so I can have my wicked way with you."

"The public restroom? Really? Where, if we're lucky, it will only stink of urinal cakes."

"You're no fun. What about a broom closet? Those are private. But we'll have to let the brooms watch."

"Liam…"

"I know, I know. This is business." He laughed. "No time for fun. I should've stayed on the boat."

Liam had a thirty-five-foot sailing yacht, and he loved to sail. The sailboat was docked down at a pricey Portland marina near the waterfront and not far from the house they'd bought recently. Liam spent a lot of time out on the water with Jack. It was something they both enjoyed, something away from the business world and all its pressures.

"Why don't you go then?" Jack said. "I can handle this. I'll meet you there later."

"No. I want to support you. This is important to you, so it's important to me."

Jack nodded, his throat tightening a little with emotion. Damn, he did love this man, though. Four years now, they had been together. Sometimes just the two of them, sometimes with a woman. They were both bi, both very open about it too. Their love had always been the core, the strongest, but even though they brought women into their relationship, they hadn't found the right woman yet. Not one who was special to both of them. Someone they both had to have in their lives forever. Much of the time, it had just been the two of them, and the women had drifted away when they couldn't compete with the love between Jack and Liam.

Or maybe it was all Jack's fault. Liam was easygoing and free with his affection and open with his feelings. He was practically a modern-day hippie who cleaned up really well. But Jack... He'd cared for the women they'd sometimes shared their lives and their beds with...but no one had really caught his heart yet.

Not the way Liam did. And that was what he wanted.

He snorted. Didn't everyone want that? He was just another greedy bastard. Always wanting more.

He pushed those thoughts away, trying to put on his calm and competent face again. After all, the local media might show up. Projecting the right image was important. It was a calculated strategy. That was another reason for the jeans and work boots. People expected billionaires to wear zillion-dollar suits made out of endangered lama eyebrows or whatever. He wasn't like that. He could clean up nice, sure, but that conspicuous consumption? That wasn't him. It never had been.

Right now, he was here in Maine to create jobs. To make money, yes, but more than anything to put people back to work in his home state.

He cleared his throat, getting a grip on his wandering thoughts. He was still curious about a few things between Liam and that woman. "Did you get her name?"

Liam looked at him as if he'd just been insulted. "Of course. I'm not slowing down in my old age. Her name is Rebecca Johnson."

"All right, old man, don't get offended. So why did you help her move her tables? She had a good spot."

"She did, but apparently you bought out more space than you needed. Surprise, surprise. She was on floor space assigned to Lighthouse. Apparently, another organizer told her to set up there. It was a mess."

Hmm. That sounded right. He might've rented more floor space than they'd strictly needed. He simply wanted to make sure this trade show went well for them and was useful for everyone attending— Lighthouse most of all. "Why didn't you tell her she could stay there? I mean, we're not even using it."

Liam's thick eyebrows shot up. "I gladly would have, but she isn't too keen on a guy named Jack Meacham." He broke out into another wide grin. "She thought I was you at first." He brushed invisible dust off his lapels. "I must look like a billionaire."

"You *are* a billionaire, you idiot."

He shrugged, for a moment seeming a little uncomfortable. Not a typical thing from Liam. "That's because I can't give it away fast enough. All I really need is my boat. And you."

Jack grunted. Liam, a romantic fool through and through. But Liam had joined the ranks of the billionaires six or seven years ago, just out of the university. He'd made a fortune on an app he'd created. It was a meditation, relaxation app, New Age-y stress relief. Totally Liam to the core.

And it had caught on big.

He frowned and glanced back at the woman much farther down the side aisle. There was far more foot traffic now, and lots of it was around the Lighthouse area, with people trying samples of fresh-baked bread, bagels, crackers, biscuits, muffins, flatbreads, brownies, pies, and of course, cookies. But the woman's simple vendor setup was getting some decent traffic too. He even overheard one attendee exclaiming over how good one of Rebecca Johnson's cookies tasted.

"Why doesn't she like me?" he asked Liam, trying not to sound petulant. "She doesn't even know me."

Liam bumped him with a shoulder. "Maybe because you, I don't know, forced her to move at the last minute because you rented too much floor space?"

"That wasn't me," he said, outraged.

Liam shrugged. Sometimes the man was so calm it was maddening.

"Maybe she doesn't know that," Liam suggested.

Damn it. He didn't really have time for this. But he supposed the different areas of their section were managing themselves well enough right now. He should go over and meet her. Not to apologize. He didn't have anything to apologize for. He'd go to see if she needed anything.

"All right," he told Liam. "Hold down the fort. I'm going to talk with her."

Liam eyed the Lighthouse tables and employees. "I don't know anything about bakeries."

Jack pointed at the box of cookies in Liam's hand and smirked. "But you certainly know cookies. Those aren't our brand. You're clearly disloyal."

"You can kiss my ass, Meacham," Liam retorted, grinning. "These were a gift. For my help. And they are really good."

"I'd ask to try one, but since they are free and

I'm heading over there right now, it will give me an excuse to be there." Jack began to walk toward the aisle leading to her booth. As he went, he waved goodbye to Liam.

Liam held up his box of cookies as if he'd just pulled Excalibur from the stone. "You enjoy your free sample. I've got an entire box. Who's laughing now?"

Jack discretely gave him the finger—this was a family venue after all—and Liam broke out in laughter.

He wandered through the people in the aisles until he reached Rebecca Johnson's booth. She was busy selling a box of her cookies to an elderly lady wearing a Red Sox hat.

Jack eyed the Cookie Nookie setup as he waited. It was strictly low budget. The logo was a decent enough design—bold lines and colors, a clear theme— but the name of her business was silly. Cookie Nookie. Who could take a place named like that seriously? It should be the name of a private lap dance room at a strip club or something.

But Rebecca Johnson was certainly attractive. Pretty enough, her body lush, curvy in all the right ways. Feminine curves that immediately caught and held the eye.

He could understand why Liam had wandered over to her in the first place. Liam loved women. He was bisexual, yes, just like Jack. But if Jack were honest, he would admit that Liam probably leaned more toward women than men on the sliding scale of attraction. Jack didn't feel threatened by this, even though he was also bi and the opposite, probably leaning more toward men on that attraction scale. He didn't feel threatened because Liam had proven over and over again how much he loved Jack. Loved everything about him, from being together drinking beers on the deck of his sailboat to scorching-hot sex in their penthouse mansion or on Jack's private plane.

Jack felt exactly the same way about him.

But this woman was cute, and those big eyes of hers were friendly...and maybe a little vulnerable. No wonder Liam had rushed to play the White Knight. Also, she had pretty lips and a dusting of freckles over a cute nose. Cute, with a sexy enough shape if you liked your women thicker. He did, and so did Liam. What was it they said? More to grapple with? Crude, but maybe true.

When she was done helping the old lady, he wandered closer.

She beamed at him, which surprised him. Hadn't Liam said she hated Lighthouse Bakery? Why was she smiling at him when he was the owner and driving force behind the venture?

"Good morning," she said, and that smile really did move her from cute into pretty-damn-attractive territory. It lit up her face, made her light brown eyes shine. "Would you like a free sample?"

"I would," he said, returning her smile. It was infectious. He looked down at the cookies and picked an oatmeal cookie. Liam was a cookie fiend. The man mainlined them like some kind of drug. But Jack actually preferred pies. Not cakes. Pies. Give him a hot apple pie with melting ice cream or a pecan pie so rich you could barely finish but always did anyway, and you could call him a happy man. So he didn't intend to be that impressed by a cookie.

He bit into it. The cookie was delicious, not overly sweet but moist, chewy, and with hints of brown sugar and cinnamon. These days, everyone began to twitch when the word *moist* was used, but damn it, the word fit. The cookie was the perfect ratio on the moist index. He took another bite just to be sure. Then another.

Then, to hell with it, he finished the cookie.

She was watching him, a smile lingering on those full lips. She handed him a napkin.

He thanked her. No wonder Liam was guarding his box of these cookies with his life.

"That was delicious," he told her. "Ever consider selling the recipe?"

She looked shocked by the question. Appalled even. "No! It's my handcrafted recipe."

Too bad. It was worth a chance. He could move a lot of those cookies when Lighthouse ramped up, and the advertising kicked in. First, Maine, then nationwide.

He reached into his back pocket, pulled out a card, and handed it to her. "If you change your mind. We could enter into some kind of deal. Generous royalties or a big lump sum payment. Whatever you'd like."

She took his card even as she was shaking her head again. "Look, I'm flattered you like them, but I don't really..." She trailed off, and her eyes widened as she read his name on the fancy gold-embossed business card. Now her gaze sharpened into knives as she glared at him. "You! You're Jack Meacham. The owner of Lighthouse Bakery!"

"Guilty as charged." He didn't know why she was so riled up. She looked as though he had just kidnapped her cat or something. He considered asking her but decided it wasn't worth his time. Liam might like her, but she clearly hated Jack's guts. "By the way, some free advice. I'd change the name of your business. Cookie Nookie is cute, but cute only goes so far in life."

She was still glaring at him. He noticed she had crushed his business card in her fist.

Jack had to bite back a surge of annoyance. What was her deal? Why was she so emotional? He'd made a business offer in good faith. Even if she spurned his offer, he didn't really want her to fail. If she changed the name of her business to something more homey and wholesome, she'd probably have every grandmother in the state banging on her shop door, buying her cookies to pass off as their own.

"You can take your *free advice*," Rebecca Johnson

snarled, "and go take a flying fuck at a rolling doughnut."

One of the women who had been sampling a cookie gasped, clutched her purse, and hurried away looking scandalized.

"See?" he chided. "That's not family-friendly."

"You... *You...*"

He sighed. "Listen. I'm sorry the event organizers made you move. I had nothing to do with it and no problem with you staying where you were."

"Well, I do!"

"You do what?"

"Have a problem staying where I was! I could smell your arrogance all the way across the aisle. And it smells like cow manure, burning tires, and turpentine!"

He burst out laughing. "That's very specific."

This woman was clearly unhinged. He'd tried to do a good thing—seeing if she needed anything, maybe checking her out because Liam was so entranced—and it bit him in the ass.

"You have a very specific stink," she assured him, nostrils flaring. "You think you can come over here and buy me out like it was nothing? As if I wasn't here first, with my own business—a successful one, thank you very much! I worked hard to make this." She waved her hands around at the cookies. "All of these recipes. They aren't made my machines and mass-baked at some industrial factory. These are baked with love!"

He rolled his eyes. "It's always people baking with love. That cliché is so tired. Can we get a new one?"

"No! And you can burn your cookies, Scrooge. Just like your heart."

He couldn't help laughing again, even though it clearly pissed her off even more. "I'm sorry, did you just call me Scrooge? And my heart is burned? What does that even mean?" He tossed his napkin in the trash. "I think we're done."

"We're most definitely done," she snapped.

He looked at her, smirking. "You missed your chance. I was certain you were going to say we were...overdone."

She closed her eyes. Her fists were clenched. He decided to leave before she started winging cookies at him.

But just because, he took out another business card and put it on the table to replace the one she'd crushed. "In case you change your mind about the recipe."

Then he turned on his heel and walked off.

He winced when he heard the swinging lid of the trashcan bang hard. He didn't need to turn around to imagine her throwing that card away as well.

Liam was eating cookies and sitting in a chair near the coffee station. He hadn't been witness to the scene.

"So?" Liam said. "Those cookies are angelic, aren't they?"

"Yeah, they are," he shot back.. "But that woman is a demon."

And crazy.

"What do you mean? Were you a jerk, Jack?"

"Hey. When am I ever a jerk?"

"Whenever you forget what a good guy you are. That's when. Do I need to go over to her and apologize?"

Jack frowned. "Don't bother. It won't help. She hates my guts. She hates Lighthouse. Nothing you could say will change that."

Liam looked disappointed...but he didn't go rushing off to apologize to her either. He must have realized that if she hated Jack, then there wasn't much hope of the three of them ever having fun together.

But seeing Liam disappointed about anything only made Jack feel bad. And feeling bad only made him feel more irritable.

Cookie Nookie. Give me a break.

So...if that was all true, why was he still thinking about her?

CHAPTER TWO

Rebecca

Two days later...

Rebecca waited impatiently as the old woman in front of her turned on her right turn blinker and then drove two entire blocks before actually slowing to a near stop and making a right turn.

Usually, she was very calm in traffic and didn't let things like that get to her. But today she had somewhere to be. She glanced at the dashboard clock again. Ten minutes until the city council meeting started. She didn't want to miss it. With her luck, they would discuss "city planning issues related to the opening of Lighthouse Bakery" right away, and she'd miss the only reason she was going.

Not that she could stop Lighthouse from opening, even if she'd wanted to. And she only kind of wanted to. Well, that wasn't exactly true. Her feelings were complex, like everything else in life. She wanted people to have jobs, and the town was excited about it too. Other businesses—coffee shops and diners—were thrilled. People making more money meant people spending more money.

But personally, she didn't need Lighthouse Bakery edging her out or undercutting her prices with the local shops and restaurants she depended on. Sure, she'd still have street traffic, but cookies were not coffee, and tourism had been down to lows the town hadn't seen since 2008. People were edgy.

So she wanted to attend this public meeting and hear what people said. She wasn't going to speak. She couldn't exactly get up there and yell about Lighthouse driving small business out of business. She would sound like a deranged hypocrite, thinking only of herself. But she would be lying if she didn't secretly hope the zoning board or whatever made life difficult for Jack Meacham and his new business venture.

She sped up as she saw the courthouse and city municipal building. Almost all the streets in Freemont were two-lane streets with not a lot of width. These downtown streets were the worst. They were even narrower because people parked on both sides of the street.

Some pedestrians saw her unmistakable Cookie Nookie mobile and waved. She waved back while trying not to speed. That was another reason she had to "drive nice," even though she was in a hurry and that old lady had been going twenty miles an hour when the posted limit was thirty.

People recognized her car. They should, it was distinctive enough. It was a 2011 Nissan Cube, painted to look like a chocolate chip cookie. It had her Cookie Nookie logo plastered all over it, along with her shop's phone number, web address, and several slogans: "Premium cookies at homemade prices" and "Fall in love with cookies all over again!"

But those weren't the most memorable things.

Mounted on top of the boxy hatchback was a big old plastic peanut butter blossom cookie with a chocolate kiss. It was silly. It was unforgettable. And right now, it was a little annoying, because one of the mounting bolts holding the chocolate kiss to the cookie frame had come loose a week ago. The whole thing rattled like a maraca as she drove along the street.

Rattling cookie aside, her car was something of a local legend. She used it every morning to make cookie deliveries to the shops and restaurants that either resold her cookies or used them in desserts like cookie sundaes and cookie skillets. She'd needed every bit of the tax write-off, so she'd decided to turn the car into a driving billboard.

Mr. Milligan, who owned the local paper, was walking toward the municipal building. He saw her, grinned and waved. He was one of her best customers, so she waved back, smiling broadly even though she didn't really feel like it. She hadn't felt like smiling since Mr. Moneybags Meacham had tried to steal her cookie recipe. Well, technically he'd offered to buy it, but she still considered it a form of theft. Theft of her cookie magic secrets. They were priceless.

Listen to you. You're growing unhinged about Jack Meacham.

Was she though? Because the guy was a snake. Or maybe he wasn't a snake, but he was certainly one of those rich guys who felt like they owned the world just because they could buy most of it. And what was he trying to pull with that jeans and work shirt outfit? Sure, he'd fooled her with it. She'd thought he was just another worker. And the fact that she'd been bamboozled and made a fool out of herself at the trade show only made her dislike him more.

The traffic on the downtown road was tight because of the meeting, the street was narrow, and most of the street parking was gone. Was she too late? Was she not going to get a parking spot in time because of the old lady...and the fact that she'd taken too much time picking out exactly the right outfit?

But as she cruised past the municipal building parking lot, she spotted an open space near the end of the lot, under a Hawthorne tree. She needed to rush in quickly and park there before someone stole her spot.

With all the cars parked on the streets, the entrance came up faster than she expected. She cleared a huge Dodge truck that was blocking out half the world. Ahead of her, an oncoming car had its blinker on, intending to turn left into the lot. She had the space to make a right turn first, and she had the right of way. But the other car seemed to realize this and sped up to turn in front of her.

She didn't back down. That guy wanted her spot, and she *needed* it.

She took the right turn, zooming into the parking lot, and cried out when she saw the back-end of a black car right in front of her.

She stomped on the brakes. Her tires screamed.

Then a loud *crunch* filled the air. It was the sound of two cars meeting unexpectedly in the night.

To add to the humiliation, the chocolate kiss came flying off the plastic peanut butter cookie on the roof and hit the other car's rear windshield. It didn't break the glass, but it rolled down to the trunk and sat there looking quite strange.

Crap. Why me? FML. FML so hard.

The car she'd rear-ended was a Mercedes Benz. She was staring right at the little unmistakable emblem along with the words Maybach and S-560.

Oh, double-shit. This was going to cost her insurance so much money. Which meant it would cost *her* so much money after they raised her rates into the stratosphere.

She closed her eyes and tried to calm herself.

Focus on the positive.

She couldn't. What was positive about rear-ending a car that cost hundreds of thousands of dollars?

No, focus on the positives! She wasn't hurt. No whiplash even. There was that.

Okay, so she had one positive and a whole long list of negatives. Including the broken, plastic chocolate kiss sitting on the trunk of the fancy car she'd just rammed.

Why on Earth had the Benz guy pulled into the parking lot and *stopped* in the entrance for heaven's sake?

As she looked around with her heart still thudding in her chest and her pulse beating in her temples, she saw the reason why. The Benz was waiting for someone else to back out of a parking space. She'd simply come around the corner too quickly, trying to beat that other driver into the parking lot. She hadn't seen the Benz until it was too late because of the big truck blocking most of her view.

Not that any of those excuses were going to matter. No, she had just committed insurance suicide. She was at fault, and she'd damaged something ridiculously expensive.

The driver-side door to the Mercedes Benz opened. A man climbed out.

The man was wearing a very expensive designer suit. He was glaring at her. Death-daggers were coming out of his eyes and stabbing her through the windshield.

Her heart sank lower than her socks when she saw the man was none other than Jack Meacham. Because of course it was. Who else would drive a car like that in a town like this?

She'd probably be forced to sell him all her recipes just to pay for the damages. Wouldn't that just be hilarious? She blinked back tears, determined not to let him see her cry. That would be salt in the wounds.

Jack Meacham adjusted his tie as he slowly walked over to her. She sat frozen in her car, clutching the wheel in a death grip. He had a fierce scowl on his face as he stopped and eyed the damage to his car. He might have big-screen handsome looks, but when he glared, it was really intimidating.

He reached out and picked up the broken chocolate kiss that was lying on the car's trunk. He held it in his hands, his expression disgusted, as if he were holding a great big dollop of poop instead of a plastic chocolate kiss.

Then he turned and walked to her window. He leaned down slowly. He lifted the plastic chocolate kiss and showed it to her.

She rolled down the window, her heart beating faster than a rabbit's.

"Are you hurt?" he asked with surprising gentleness, even though those gray-blue eyes were sharp as flint.

"No. Are you?"

"No." He held out the chocolate kiss to her. "I think this is yours."

"Oh…" she said. "I wondered where that went."

He stared at her.

She tried to look innocent, as if she hadn't just

rammed his car. It hadn't been on purpose. She might think he was an arrogant jerk, but she didn't want to damage his property. She wasn't *completely* crazy.

He kept holding the plastic kiss, staring at her as if she were an alien in a cookie-painted spaceship. Gingerly, she reached out, took the chocolate kiss, and placed it beside her on the passenger seat. It had caused enough trouble for today.

Jack was still looking at her. "So, what now? Are you going to claim I backed into you?"

"What?" she squawked, outraged. The absolute nerve of this man! "Of course not!"

He nodded, his scowl softening a little. "I suppose I should call the police—"

Rebecca burst into tears.

She hated herself for crying, especially in front of him, but all the stress and worry of the last few months had caught up to her. It was magnified by this crash fiasco. She should never have come here tonight. Then this disaster wouldn't have happened. She cursed herself for being such a busybody when it came to Lighthouse Bakery.

And she cursed Jack Meacham for being in that

car that she just so happened to accidentally smash into. Especially after he was such a...such a belligerent cad to her at the trade show. As if she was wrong or bad for refusing to sell him her best recipes!

Jack was watching her warily. He was still scowling, but his face paler, unsettled by her sudden emotional breakdown. He'd raised his right hand toward her as if he half intended to reach through the window and pat her. Well, she didn't want his reassurances. Especially since he was the cause of so much of her misery.

She sobbed harder, her nose running, her mascara running. Someone behind them honked angrily. She had to restrain herself from grabbing the plastic chocolate kiss and hurling at whatever jerk was honking at her in her most vulnerable time. But she didn't. Because that wouldn't be good for business.

Jack turned his scowl away from her and focused it on the impatient driver. With curt gestures, he waved the other car around them and into the parking lot. The impatient driver zoomed past and pulled into the spot Rebecca had been rushing to get.

Now her spot was gone. That made her cry

harder. The more she tried to stop, the more she couldn't.

Through a bleary curtain of tears, she noticed the passenger-side door of the Benz open and Liam step out. He was wearing...jeans, flip flops, a long silver necklace with a yin-yang symbol, and a T-shirt with a rock and roll band on it. The exact opposite of what she'd last seen him wearing at the trade show.

He hurried over to her car, coming to the passenger-side window. "What the hell are you doing, Jack?" he growled at the other man. "You made her cry."

Jack looked stunned. "Me? I only said we should call the police! Then she started crying. What is she, a fugitive?"

"I'm not a fugitive!" she said. Or that's what she tried to say. With the sobbing and the snuffling, it came out rather garbled and less forceful than she intended.

"No, love," Liam said to her with a reassuring smile. "We know you aren't a fugitive. Because this is the least inconspicuous getaway car in the world."

She burst out laughing. That helped her get herself under some sort of control. She started digging in her handbag for some tissues. And maybe a bag to put over her head to hide her shame.

Jack cleared his throat. "Listen, I'll call the police—"

"We don't need police," Liam said, cutting him off with a pointed glare. "We'll sort this out between us."

Jack's expression was dubious and a bit annoyed. But he didn't say anything, which was perfect. She only wanted to talk with Liam.

Liam opened the passenger door and leaned inside. "Don't worry, Rebecca. This looks like a bigger deal than it really is—" He suddenly noticed the big plastic chocolate kiss sitting on the passenger seat. He stopped talking to goggle at it. "What is that? A giant poop emoji?"

That surprised another half-coughing, half-sobbing laugh out of her. But at least she'd managed to stop the waterworks and focus on something else other than the wreckage of her car and her life.

She had Liam to thank for that. Not Jack, who was a jerk and a total clod.

"No," she finally said, shaking her head but

eyeing the chocolate kiss dubiously. Because the more she thought about it, the more the thing *did* sort of look like a poop emoji. All it needed was the happy face. "It's a chocolate kiss. From the big cookie on the roof."

"I see," he said, but from his tone, he didn't. "Is there a reason it's riding in the passenger seat without being buckled in?"

"When she rear-ended us," Jack said sourly, "that thing flew off her car and hit the Benz."

Liam nodded, plopped down in the passenger seat beside her, and took her hand.

Her eyes widened in surprise. In fact, she was so surprised that she didn't even pull her hand away. It was quite forward of him to touch her…but part of her really liked it. And she liked the way he was looking at her right now, even though she was a tear-stained wreck. He was watching her with sympathy and caring in his eyes. As if her feelings mattered.

That was way better than Jack Meacham, who watched her as if she was some strange alien species that might not be right in the head. What a jerk.

"Rebecca," Liam said and then paused. "May I call you Rebecca?"

She nodded.

His grin was brilliant. It really lit up his eyes and made her stomach flutter. It made her tighten and ache somewhere else too. She shifted a little in her seat, willing herself not to be aroused. Who heard of melting into a horny mess just because of a smile, especially after a wrenching tear-fest?

But oh, what a smile.

"Thank you," Liam continued. At her driver's side door, she heard Jack snort with a mix of amusement and scorn. What a jerk. She ignored him. She was focused on Liam. He was clearly the better man. She wondered what he saw in Jack Meacham since it was obvious they were together.

If possible, the wattage on Liam's smile intensified. "It's a cliché, but I'm going to say it anyway. Accidents happen. Tell you what. You're probably worried about your insurance going through the roof after this. Am I right?"

She bit her lip and nodded, fighting back fresh tears. She was a fool. She shouldn't be so grateful that he understood. But she was.

"Completely understandable," Liam said. "Don't

worry about it. We're not calling the cops. We're not even going to report this to insurance companies—"

"Oh, we're not?" Jack growled.

"No, we're *not*," Liam replied, his smile vanishing for a moment as he glared at Jack. "We're going to pay to have her front end fixed. And we're going to pay to have our bumper fixed. Because we all know shit happens. Don't we, Jack?"

She turned to glance up at Jack. He had locked eyes with Liam, his handsome face darkened with a scowl. He clearly didn't like what Liam was proposing.

It was silly, but a part of her wanted to stick her tongue out at him. So there, jerkface. How do you like that? At least someone was a gentleman.

Even though this was all her fault to begin with...

Slowly, Jack turned that scowl from Liam to her. She lifted her chin, not looking away. He could glare all he wanted. She refused to burst into tears again.

Finally, his lips curved up into a wry smirk. "Fine. It's not like I can't afford it."

Listen to Mr. Moneybags Meacham. Taunting her with how rich he was. The man was simply intolerable.

Beside her, Liam nodded. He was looking at her again, and when she met his hazel eyes with the amber ring around the pupil, her heart began to beat faster, and she sucked in a wavering breath.

"So don't worry about that anymore," Liam told her. "Now, with that taken care of, let's move our cars so we don't miss this meeting. Since that's why we're all here tonight."

She felt her cheeks and the back of her neck grow hot. Were they wondering why she was coming to this city council meeting in the first place? After all, she didn't have any business on the agenda. Then again, she owned a main-street business—if only a tiny one—so she had a right to stick her nose into city business. If she wanted to. So there. Take that, Jack Meacham.

One problem still remained.

"There are no more parking spaces," she pointed out.

The parking space she'd been zooming after had been taken. She'd helplessly watched that happen.

"You probably can't see it from there," Liam said

gently. "But the space we were waiting on is still open."

She shifted in her seat enough to see. The car they had been waiting for had backed out and left, but maybe because of the accident, no one had slipped into the empty slot.

"It's open," Jack said, "because everyone else wants to stay far, far away from all the drama."

Liam glared at him. Even she was impressed by the scowl. Liam might be handsome and charming and warm, but his glares were cold enough to freeze a lake on a hot summer day. "Accidents *happen*." Then Liam's glare vanished like smoke when he turned his gaze back to her. "Why don't you park in the space we were waiting for?" He glowered at Jack again. "Jack will be happy to find another place for our car, won't you, Jack?"

She looked up at Jack, biting the inside of her cheek to not smile at how hard Jack Meacham was clenching his jaw.

"So, I guess I'll move my car," Jack growled. "Even though I probably won't find another parking spot for miles."

"Our hero," Liam said, grinning again. The way

he could turn that panty-melting smile on and off had to be Liam's superpower. "I'll stay here and keep Rebecca company. If she's agreeable, that is."

"You're not coming with me?" Jack sounded surprised.

"Why would I want to walk all that way? Besides, I should stay with Rebecca. Smooth over all this drama you caused." His eyes narrowed at Jack. "Be a *gentleman*." And wham, that charming smile was back when he looked back at Rebecca. "Besides, what man wouldn't love a pretty lady on his arm?"

She flushed. *Be careful*, she warned herself. *This guy is dangerously charming.*

But even though she knew that, she was still susceptible to every bit of it. It was all biology. A primal response from her body to his, especially with them so close. Not that things would go anywhere. The guy was partners with Jack Meacham (and no accounting for taste), so Liam was gay and clearly not interested in her despite the charm offensive. But even so, she was still a sucker for charm and flattery.

Meanwhile, Jack Meacham looked as if his head was about to explode while he'd been listening to

Liam's words. "*She* crashed into *me.*"

Liam waved a hand as if unconcerned with minor details. "Don't worry, we'll save you a seat inside. Now would you kindly move the car so Rebecca can park? I don't want someone to suddenly get bold and take that spot after all of this."

Jack made a show of a deeply sarcastic bow. "Your wish is my command, sir. Just let me kick some of the wreckage and debris from my Mercedes out of the way."

"Great," Liam replied brightly. "We'll wait here while you do *and* thank our lucky stars no one was hurt *and* we'll marvel over how modern technology can repair cars as good as new." He winked at her. "Isn't that right, Rebecca?"

She found herself breaking out in a grin. "That's right. It's amazing."

Jack looked at Liam. Then he looked at her. And finally, he turned on his heel and walked back to the Benz while shaking his head.

They watched as he got in and slammed the door. Jack pulled forward in the Benz, swinging around to another row of the parking lot. She put her car in drive and edged her way into the last empty parking slot.

They caught sight of the Benz rolling past from the opposite way. The rear end was a bit damaged, the bumper clearly crimped. Even though the damage looked minor, on a Mercedes, it would probably cost more money to fix than her car's original sticker price.

Again, a surge of gratitude to Liam swept through her. For not calling the cops or involving insurance. For freaking paying for the damages...*and the damages to her car*! That kind of generosity hit her harder and deeper than even Liam's charm offensive.

She opened her mouth to thank Liam again, but Jack squealed the tires of the Benz as he pulled out of the parking lot and onto the street. He was letting them both know exactly what he thought of this situation.

Liam snorted. "Don't mind him. He only acts like a total bastard when he's worried. He has a soft, gooey caramel center. I promise."

She didn't really believe that, but she wasn't going to call Liam out on it. It would be rude. "Why is he worried?"

"He always worries. This whole project, this

factory their building here, it means everything to him. Even though everything's going smoothly, he's worried there will be some hitch tonight with the city council." Liam shook his head and shrugged. "I'm trying to teach him to be more Zen."

"I see..." She hated to admit it but hearing that made it a little more difficult to dislike the man. Not much, but a little. Because it made him seem a little more human.

As she turned, she caught a glimpse of herself in the rearview mirror. She winced. Tears had done her no favors. "I need a moment to...fix my face."

"Go right ahead." He opened the car door. "Since Jack didn't pick up any of the broken plastic despite bitching about it, I'll get it off the pavement while you do what you need to do."

She fixed her makeup as quickly as she could. Liam picked up the few pieces of broken plastic from her busted headlight and turn signal. Then he waited patiently for her to finish, which made him some kind of saint in her book.

Was this guy really male? He seemed so kind, patient, and considerate. Or was it simply because he was gay? She didn't know, but she found herself really wishing he was straight. That wasn't fair at all. She hated herself for thinking that. But part of her—a selfish, greedy part—thought it all the same.

She got out of the car and smoothed her dress, wishing she'd worn something that showed a little more cleavage. God, she was an idiot.

Liam held out his arm for her to take. She took his arm, both nervous and excited.

He took one last look at her vehicle. "I love your car, by the way. It's adorable. Don't worry, we'll get it fixed up like new. Even the chocolate kiss will be right as rain again."

Rebecca choked back another flood of gratitude, grateful tears, and...and she didn't know what else. She really liked this man. Maybe he was simply charming her. Some men were actually incapable of turning off their charm, no matter what. But she was enjoying every bit of his attention, basking in the warmth of his gaze. And that smile... It made her want all sorts of naughty things she really shouldn't be thinking about right before a city council meeting. Or with a man who was clearly already dedicated to another.

Even if his taste in partners is appalling...

She glanced at the big plastic cookie display mounted on the top of the car. "It looks so strange without the chocolate kiss on top. But...does the kiss really look like...the poop emoji?"

He chuckled. "No, not really. I only said that because I wanted to see you smile." His own smile blazed away. "Now come on. We don't want to miss too much of the fascinating world of local politics."

She laughed and let him escort her into the big concrete municipal building.

And Jack Meacham was nowhere to be seen.

CHAPTER THREE

Liam

They missed the first ten minutes or so of the council meeting, but that didn't matter. Liam found them a spot to sit midway down the seats on the right side of the large meeting room. He claimed an extra seat for Jack for whenever he managed to get back here.

He felt a twinge of regret that he'd goaded Jack into roaming the city looking for a place to park. But let's face it, Jack had been acting like a jerk. Yeah,

Rebecca had hit the car. So what? It was an accident. Life was full of them. What the hell good was being rich if you couldn't use your money to fix things? To make life better. For yourself. For the people you cared for. For the world.

That was how he thought, anyway. He'd never been comfortable with the amount of money his wildly popular app had made. He had some kind of survivor's guilt over it. All his life, he'd lived a middle class—or maybe lower middle class—existence. But after the truckloads of money started rolling it, he'd been staggered. Then he'd wondered what to do with it all.

Yeah, yeah. It was a problem ninety-nine percent of America, not to mention the rest of the world, would love to have. He was deeply aware of that.

But that also meant it was nothing to him to pay to fix Rebecca's car and the Benz without involving insurance companies or the cops and putting an accident report on her record. That would cost her money for years. It annoyed him that Jack had even considered it. Sure, one of Jack's favorite cars was a little dinged up, but damn it, Jack could buy himself six more tomorrow morning and not even miss the money.

Hell, Liam could do the same. It made him feel both good and guilty to see the gratitude in Rebecca's eyes. Because paying to make this right was nothing to either of them, but it was everything to her.

He glanced at the woman beside him. At least he'd managed to set things right and bring a smile back to those full lips of hers. She was still a little pale and blotchy from crying, but now she was watching the council go over city business as if it was actually fascinating instead of one of the most boring things Liam had ever endured.

He'd much rather spend his time looking at her.

Liam grinned. Since the moment he'd tried one of her cookies, she'd won his heart. Okay, that was an exaggeration. But there was something about her that simply appealed to him. Maybe appealed to him on a molecular level. It was the same powerful, uncompromising way that Jack appealed to him. A magnetism. A link that couldn't be denied.

All right. He was being a bit over the top, maybe even cheesy. Hell, he was a romantic, even though it wasn't cool for men to be that way. Not too much anyway. Jack teased him about it sometimes, saying it was a good thing Liam still liked action movies and college football or they wouldn't have anything in common. An ex-body-boarding beach bum from the California Coast and a son of New York City. Who would've thought?

The council had moved to discussing the installation of a red light-slash-speed radar camera at one of the downtown Freemont intersections. Great. Jack would love that. Those radar cameras had given him more than a dozen tickets in the last few years. Speaking of astronomical insurance rates...

He stole another glance at Rebecca, wondering why she had come tonight. Was she simply one of those civic-minded people you ran into every so often, as strange as that concept seemed. Personally, he hated politics. It seemed to bring out the worst in people—even otherwise good people.

But no, he didn't want to think about boring and disgusting politics. He wanted to think about the beautiful woman sitting next to him. He found it hard to look at Rebecca and not feel a telling tightening in his groin, his cock stirring with interest. Because she really was stunning. And she really did have...hmm, how to say it tactfully? She had a bust of a very respectable size. He bit his cheek to stop a smile at how silly that sounded. Still, viewing from the side—and not staring, which was a challenge, because he was a man who loved women after all—her bust truly was very…noticeable.

Despite his attempt to be tactful, images pushed their way into his brain. Fantasies of him kissing along that curve of neck where she'd swept her hair back over her shoulders. Kissing that creamy skin while fondling that closest breast, feeling the weight and heft of it. Stroking his thumb over the tip, teasing her nipple even through the fabric of the dress. He wanted to hear a moan escape those full, almost pouty lips of hers. He wanted her to close her eyes, giving in to the pleasure of every kiss, of every caress, as he made her feel like a goddess—

Aaaand, wonderful. Now he was hard as a rock. Like some punk teenager in math class daydreaming about blowjobs.

He chuckled and shifted in his seat, trying to hide the evidence of his arousal. Rebecca glanced at him, her cute face curious. Liam was saved from having to explain why he was chuckling by the sudden appearance of Jack.

Jack still looked annoyed as he found them and stopped in the aisle. A scowl was still on his face, and he looked ready to read Liam the riot act. Liam wasn't worried. Jack deserved everything coming to him tonight. Why? Because he'd completely forgotten to act like the gentleman Liam knew him to be.

Besides, he would make it up to Jack later. Speaking of blowjobs, he'd give Jack one that would have the man's eyes rolling back in his head and his knees giving out.

Jack entered their row, moving toward the seat on Liam's right that he'd saved for him. Liam realized he probably should've saved Jack the aisle seat, but that had been the seat Rebecca had chosen. So Liam had to shift again, turning his legs and hips to let Jack past. But unfortunately, the movement really drew attention to his crotch...and the bulge of his cock straining against his jeans.

Oh, and of course Rebecca had turned her head as she moved to let Jack down the aisle. And of course she ended up looking right at the bold evidence of

Liam's excitement.

Because of course that happened.

Her eyes widened, but she didn't look up to meet his gaze. Instead, she very pointedly began staring at the city council members as if they were the most fascinating things she'd ever seen.

Wonderful. Now she probably thought he was a total freak who got aroused by city council meetings. What the hell kind of kink was that?

But it was all so funny that he laughed aloud. He couldn't help it.

Jack—and several surrounding people—turned to glare at him.

"What, are you crazy?" Jack whispered as he settled into the seat beside Liam. "You're embarrassing me."

"Sorry," he said, not feeling sorry in the least. "I got a little excited."

Jack grunted and turned his attention back to the boring meeting. Liam forced himself not to risk any more looks Rebecca's way. At least for now. He didn't want to make her uncomfortable.

It was difficult, though. He *wanted* to look at her.

He wanted to hear her voice. He wished they were somewhere else. Somewhere he could get to talk with her. Get to know more about her.

God, he was smitten.

It had been a while since he'd felt this way toward a woman. How long ago had their last ménage been? Two years? That had been a New York defense attorney named Layla. The three-way relationship had lasted half a year or so—hot as hell, but Layla had been worried about her professional relationship and "non-normative sexual escapades." And since Liam and Jack were in love and that was non-negotiable, she had called things off.

Well, remembering the past was enough to kill his hard-on. So there was that.

But he did catch Rebecca stealing another look at his crotch. She did a whole routine of stretching...glancing around...and throwing a side glance at his junk.

It was adorable.

If she was interested, he was more than happy to show her to her heart's content.

"Which brings us to item ten on the agenda,"

one of the city council people said. "Addressing any issues with city services and resources, including increased traffic, from the Lighthouse Bakery Company and their factory opening next month. I'd like to invite Mr. Jack Meacham to lead off the public discussion."

Jack leaned over and whispered to Liam. "Wish me luck with Councilman Grumpy Cat," he said. He stood, bringing a Spanish-leather portfolio with him as he made his way to the aisle again.

Liam did as he was asked, wishing the man he loved all the luck in the world as he addressed the city council. Jack's nickname for the councilman was meant in fun, but the guy actually did have a face that reminded them both of those grumpy cat memes on the Internet. It still would've been rather unkind to point that out, except that when they'd met the councilman at a city fundraiser, he'd actually been wearing a T-shirt with the iconic cat on it. All three of them had laughed, and Sam Steine, the real name of Councilman Grumpy Cat, had told them his granddaughter had already pointed out the resemblance. Mr. Steine was actually the complete opposite of grumpy once you got to talking to him. He was very warm, very friendly.

It went to show you that you couldn't judge books by the cover or people by their faces. Jack had a bit of resting bitch face himself. It was probably one of the things that rubbed Rebecca's fur the wrong way.

He hoped that somehow Rebecca got a chance to see the softer, kinder side of Jack. So far, both of them had gotten off on the wrong foot with each other. First, Jack had tried to buy her secret recipes. Liam might not be a foodie or even in the food industry aside from providing free taste-testing, but even he was bright enough to know Jack had walked into a minefield with that one.

And now there was this accident, making things tense between them.

He watched as Jack launched into his presentation, outlining the number of expected employees, utility needs, first responder access, and projected tax revenue for the city. Jack was never boring—at least not to Liam. He had a commanding presence, a focused intensity, especially when he was talking about this project that was near and dear to his heart. By the time he was done, he even had some of the council members clapping.

"He's good at that," Rebecca leaned in and whispered.

"He's a total pro."

She nodded, but she wasn't smiling. She was watching Jack closely. Almost as if she was evaluating him. Or *re*evaluating him.

Liam had caught the scent of her perfume when she leaned close. Something light and flowery. Not too strong, but damn was it enticing. He had to hold himself in check, keeping himself from leaning in for another, deeper inhale.

After all, he didn't want to freak her out, sniffing at her like some kind of hound dog. Apparently, she'd decided to ignore any earlier awkwardness from spotting his arousal, so he especially didn't want her feeling weird and uncomfortable again.

Mostly, he wanted to keep her smiling. Seeing her cry had been like a punch to the balls. Liam and Jack were going to share some words later about that scene. Even though he knew it had been an understandable storm-burst of emotion on her part (especially if she was afraid of how much it would cost her), he didn't appreciate Jack not being the first one to console her. Instead, Jack had looked as if he believed she was crying on purpose. As if to emotionally manipulate him or something.

Jack finished addressing the city council. He took a few questions from them, but it was clear he had a friendly audience. Jack had known going in that the city council was excited about the jobs and revenue Lighthouse would bring to the area just outside of Portland, between small-town Fremont and Maine's biggest city. For tax purposes, the factory would be zoned in Freemont's municipal area. This was nothing but a formality. A final chance for the public to make any objections known. But Jack had assured Liam that no one would be opposed to a bakery, even an industrial one.

After answering a few questions, Jack headed back to his seat beside Liam. Liam rather liked sitting between Jack and Rebecca. Either direction he turned, he had something sexy to look at. How could he complain about that?

Soon, the city council meeting was over. The room filled with conversation as people headed for the door. The three of them left too. Rebecca led the way.

Outside again, she turned to Liam, smiling a little. "Well, I guess I should be going. Thanks again for giving me your parking spot. And…for everything else."

"Our pleasure," Liam said. He glanced at Jack. "I'll walk Rebecca to her car if she doesn't mind." He couldn't help but grin at Jack. "How far away did you park?"

"What felt like five miles off in that direction," Jack groused, waving a hand eastward.

Rebecca looked guilty. Liam didn't want all the progress he'd made with her to go to waste because Jack couldn't keep from exaggerating.

"So, a couple of blocks away?" he prodded. "Great. You go get the car and pick me up. I'll walk the lady to her car. Everyone will be happy."

"*I'm* not happy about being the valet," Jack retorted.

"Two out of three people happy is good enough for me."

Rebecca was glancing back and forth between them with a small smile on her face and her eyes a bit wide as they bantered. Liam hoped she would see another side of Jack. Maybe a hint of the fun guy who was hiding under the uptight, humorless business facade he'd been wearing these last few months. Besides, giving Jack a hard time might keep her from dwelling on the accident.

"Yeah," Jack said with a hint of the old scowl. "If I'm mugged and kidnapped and sold into slavery, you'll regret being so glib."

"I will be. Completely heartbroken. And shocked, since this isn't exactly a high-crime neighborhood. But I promise I'll wait at least six months before replacing you with an up-and-coming exotic dancer named Enrique."

Rebecca burst out laughing, her pretty eyes shining.

Good. That was what he'd been hoping for. He loved making her laugh. It was like a miniature high. It pulled the same rush of endorphins he got when he made Jack laugh.

Well, *that* said something, didn't it?

"You would *not* replace him with an exotic male dancer," she said, punching Liam on the shoulder. "You're terrible."

He liked that too. The casual contact. The teasing. As if she was comfortable with it. Comfortable with him.

"For once, Ms. Johnson and I are in complete agreement," Jack said.

Liam threw up his hands. "You're right, you're right. Enrique cannot replace you, Jack. But lucky for me, I'm bisexual, so I'll get Monique from that strip club near the turnpike. She may be a gold-digger, but I'll give her your private jet to keep her happy. See? It all works out in the end."

Rebecca covered her mouth on another laugh.

Jack looked amused as he snorted and shot back, "Then I guess I can die happy. I'm off to collect the car. Like your personal parking valet." He glanced at Rebecca. His expression was a little tense, rather formal, but at least he wasn't scowling at her. "Ms. Johnson. I hope we can meet again under better circumstances."

She nodded, watching him as he walked down the sidewalk toward the main street. Liam guessed that she didn't know how to respond to Jack when he was actually acting somewhat polite. Of course, he could smack the man for alluding to the earlier accident and bringing it to mind again. He'd give Jack grief for it later.

Rebecca looked at him...and looked away again. He suspected what she wanted to ask him but was too polite to do so.

"Go ahead and ask," he prompted gently. "I promise it takes a hell of a lot to offend me. Satisfy your curiosity."

She blushed. He felt a thrill seeing that blush tint her cheeks pink. Why? Was it because he could cause a reaction in her...and that boded well for causing *other* reactions in her? He could only fantasize. Like bringing a blush to the creamy skin of her ample chest when he made her come, using his tongue, his fingers, his cock, driving her wild—

Again, he struggled to rein himself in. The sudden surge of lust was almost overwhelming. Whatever else this woman was, he couldn't deny the powerful urges she stirred in him. Urges she ignited without even seeming to be aware of it. But good lord, she was driving him crazy. In the best way possible. Just being this close to her had his cock half stiff and aching with need.

"Oh, okay," she said, brushing her hair behind her ear. "I was just surprised when you said you were bi. I mean, bisexual. You said it when you were teasing Jack." She shook her head and glanced away. "I don't mean to make a big deal about it. It's probably rude of me to say anything."

He chuckled. "No, it's not rude. And I'm not embarrassed by it. It's just the way I'm built. I'm just lucky to have found someone like Jack who feels the same way. We're two of a kind."

She raised her eyebrows. "Really? Because you seem like complete opposites."

"Okay, you got me. We *are* different. But we complement each other perfectly." He caught himself before saying anything else. Such as how they were both completely down with ménage relationships. And maybe she was curious about that?

Because he would love to satisfy her curiosity.

But no, he held his tongue. Coming on that strong was a good way to get zapped by a Taser or called a "masher" while being smacked with a handbag. Masher was a term he'd picked up watching old, black-and-white TV shows, referring to a man who thought his advances were irresistible to women.

He was no masher. No matter how much he wanted to rush forward, he needed to take his time and do this right. Especially with Jack having such a stick up his ass about a little ding on the bumper of his car.

They walked together to where her cookie car was parked. Neither of them said much, but the silence wasn't uncomfortable. When she opened her car door, he put a hand on her arm and stopped her. He wasn't ready to let her go yet. And from the look on her face, she wasn't ready to leave him yet either.

"So," he said, looking into her eyes. "Did you find out everything you wanted to know tonight?"

"What do you mean?" she asked, her face paling a little.

He figured she was trying to buy time for a good answer. He understood. They'd just met, after all. But he wanted the truth. He wanted to know her real thoughts and feelings. It was important to him.

"Why did you come tonight?" he continued, softening the question with a smile. "I find politics the worst. Local politics especially." He raised a hand as if confessing guilt. "I know, I know, that's supposed to be the most important kind. But I've never liked how politics brings out the worst in people. I wouldn't be here at all if it weren't for Jack."

"You only came to support him?"

"Exactly. I came because I want him to succeed and be happy." He looked at her. "But running into you made things so much more interesting."

She glanced away. "You mean, *me* running into *you*."

"If you want to get technical. But let's leave that in the past where it belongs. I'm more interested in something else. Like why you came tonight. Do you usually attend these meetings?"

He was fishing. He hoped she'd say or hint at something like how she'd wanted to see them again after the trade show. Or at least wanted to see *him* again, since Jack seemed to rub her exactly the wrong way.

But that was okay. They would work on that. Together.

Instead of answering right away, she bit her lip. She looked down the street, seeming unsure. Hesitant.

After a long pause, she lifted her chin and met his gaze again. "Because I'm worried about my business."

He nodded, even though that surprised him. He respected her even more for being blunt. He liked people who were honest. Honest with themselves. Honest with the world.

"Why are you worried?" he asked gently.

"Isn't it obvious? I sell cookies. Your big bakery is going to flood the supermarkets and maybe even the restaurants with product. Places I sell my cookies. I'm a very small business. I can't compete with your economies of scale and all of that. I have exactly one part-time employee to work weekends. Of course, I'm worried."

Well, he'd certainly been wrong about her hoping to see him again. Instead, she was terrified she would be driven out of business. He had to say something to put her mind at ease.

"First of all, it's not my bakery. I might be with Jack, but I made all my money on phone apps. If it weren't for this dream of Jack's, I'd be on my sailboat, touring the coastline all the way from Canada to the

Caribbean. So believe me when I say I understand. I understand why you're worried."

She snorted, frowning. "Look, I don't mean to be rude, but do you? You just told me you spend your time on a yacht or whatever. I spend most of my time baking, covered in flour, sweating in the heat of the ovens. Or cleaning things. There is so much cleaning." She took a deep breath. "This is very real to me. And I'm not sure it is to you."

Ouch. But how could he be angry with that? She was telling him the truth, or at least explaining what was perfectly valid from her point of view. He also liked that she wasn't trying to sugarcoat it either. It was true. He was very well off. Money wasn't exactly something he'd chased, but it had been a very long time since he'd had to worry about anything from healthcare to retirement and everything in-between.

"I think you have a fair point."

She eyed him uncertainly. "You do?"

"Of course. I do have a solution, though."

"What is it?" She sounded a little suspicious.

He smiled. "This doesn't work for everyone, but a long time ago, when I was still a kid, I taught myself to stop worrying about everything. It's not easy, but it's very freeing if you can pull it off. That doesn't mean you don't act, but negative emotions, pessimistic thinking, they drag you down, kill your happiness, destroy your energy." He held up a hand when she opened her mouth, looking like she meant to protest. "Again, I'm not saying it is easy. I've been trying to teach Jack the same thing since I first met him. But even trying to do it will help you."

She sighed. "I mean, that sounds good, but does anyone on Earth actually achieve it? I mean, outside of some monastery in China somewhere."

"Probably not, but remember, it is the journey, not the destination." He grinned wider. "I got that off an inspirational calendar." He shrugged. "It seemed to fit."

That got her giggling, and the tension eased. He pushed on because he wasn't done. "I promise you, Jack's not out to hurt your business. He just wants to bring new jobs and money into this community. He's very passionate about that."

Even as he explained, he knew he was going to have to lean on Jack to be careful with how he ran

Lighthouse. Jack was not a cutthroat guy, but her worries were not beyond the realm of possibility. In business, there could be all kinds of collateral damage.

She looked at him with wide, vulnerable eyes. She didn't say anything. Maybe she didn't believe him. Maybe she believed every word.

He wanted to kiss her.

So damn badly.

Would that make her believe him? And what would she do? Slap him? Kick him in the balls? He'd deserve it.

But a kiss from her would almost be worth the risk. That was unless she told him that he was a jerk and told him to get lost and that she never wanted to see him again.

No, better to keep things slow and steady. Flirt like hell, let her know he was interested, and leave it at that.

Besides, he needed to talk with Jack. Let the other man know what he was feeling. His interest in Rebecca had only gotten stronger since they'd met at the trade show.

"I'd better let you get going," he said softly.

"Goodnight, Rebecca."

"Goodnight. And look, I'm sorry to get so heavy at the end. But you asked."

"I did ask. Thank you for telling me."

"Are you...are you going to tell Jack what I said?"

"I will, unless you don't want me to. Then I won't."

"Don't. I don't want him taking pity on me."

But the way she said it, he could tell she was torn. She also didn't want pride to cost her the business she'd built. His heart went out to her.

"All right. Tell you what. I'll keep my mouth shut unless you change your mind." He grinned at her. "Then I'll use my *special* influence. It never fails."

"Thank you." She hesitated again, her gaze roaming over his face as if she were searching for something. Or evaluating how much she could trust him, whether or not he was a good man. Then, without another word, she got into her car and shut the door. He moved out of the way and watched as she drove off.

She waved to him.

He waved back, his thoughts all spinning in his

head. Tonight had been a night to remember. But he wasn't sure if all of this was moving toward a good ending or a bad one.

Jack pulled up in the Benz a few minutes later. Liam climbed into the passenger seat and shut the door. Jack raced out of the parking lot.

Neither of them said anything. Liam had too much to think about. Especially how to break it to Jack that he didn't want his lover's new pet project driving Rebecca out of business. If Rebecca asked for his help, that was. Aside from being a terrible thing, that would kill any chance Liam or Jack would have with her. He didn't want to push Jack on this, but Liam knew what he wanted.

He wanted Rebecca. He wanted Jack.

He wanted the three of them together.

Now he had to find a way to make that happen.

CHAPTER FOUR

Jack

"I want her," Liam said, looking straight into his eyes.

Jack took a deep breath, telling himself to hold his temper. He bought himself some time with a slow sip of his morning dark roast coffee, no sugar, no cream.

What the hell was going on in his life right now? Liam *wanted* the woman who had flipped out just because Jack made a completely legitimate offer to buy one of her recipes—which was a damn compliment! And then she rammed his Mercedes Benz.

Yeah, maybe it had been an accident. Or maybe she was a lunatic.

Hell, she was attractive enough, so he couldn't blame Liam there. Maybe she wouldn't end up walking a Paris runway, but she had a kind of "girl-next-door," understated and sexy charm he couldn't deny. She might be Liam's type, but Jack was not convinced. So she was cute. So she had big boobs, wide hips compared to her waist, and an alluring shape. So what?

He hadn't expected Liam to fall so hard for her. Why *this* girl out of all the women out there?

Even so, Jack knew he needed to be careful here. He warned himself not to blow this off or deny Liam's feelings.

Still, this was Liam. The man very much liked to go with the flow. He didn't usually make these kinds of proclamations. So when he did, Jack sat up and took notice.

"You want her," he finally repeated. Slowly, giving Liam time to take it back. "News flash, she hates my guts."

"She does not. And if she does, it's your fault for acting like an asshole."

He slammed his coffee down in outrage, sloshing the hot liquid over the side. He gritted his teeth and swallowed the curse on his lips.

Liam was eyeing him, clearly not happy either. Great. "So what? Now you're pissed at me? Because I'm not head over heels for this girl you like?"

He'd almost said "this girl you want to fuck" but changed his mind at the last minute. That wasn't fair. He didn't need to prove Liam right by acting like an asshole right now.

"This lady I like is a good person."

"Just because she laughs at your jokes and blushes when you smile doesn't make her a good person, Liam."

"Give me a break. Did you roll out of bed on the wrong side this morning or what? I thought you'd be in a better mood today and it'd be a good time for an honest talk."

"Oh, you mean opposed to last night, when the entire back-end of my Benz was crushed by a car painted like a cookie, with the words *Cookie Nookie* painted all over it, and a giant plastic cookie on top?"

"You know what, Jack? You can be a real dick sometimes." Liam glared at him. He leaned back against the counter, a scowl on his handsome face. A face that was usually so happy. Or at least calm.

Poor fool. He must really have it bad for her.

"Listen," Jack said, taking a deep breath. He let out a sigh. "Maybe I am acting like a dick. Maybe I'm not." Thinking back on his behavior, he was pretty sure Liam was right. He hadn't meant to make her burst into tears last night. *That* had made him feel like a dick. "The point is, I have this huge factory grand opening in less than a month. I don't have time for a woman right now. Even if she was someone we had a chance with."

"You don't think we have a chance with Rebecca?"

"Weren't you paying attention? She doesn't like me. At all. Zero percent."

"Because you were acting like an arrogant jerk who swooped in and tried to steal her recipes. I don't know anything about baking, but I'm guessing that's like the Holy Grail for bakers. Double Super Top Secret stuff. We won't even go into the part where you made her cry and tried to put the law on her."

"Put the law on her?" He could feel his eyes bulging with outrage. For a moment, he couldn't even form more words. "Am I in the twilight zone? Have I died and gone to the insane part of Hell? I wasn't trying to get her arrested *or* make her cry. And I did *not* try and steal anything! I complimented her on her cookies by trying to buy the recipe. It was a compliment!"

Liam snorted and walked over to get himself more coffee. Jack watched—breathing fast and trying to calm down—as Liam poured in half a cow's worth of cream. He couldn't believe they were actually fighting over this. This...woman.

How long had it been since that had happened? Had it ever happened before? He didn't think so. Wonderful.

Liam walked back over and took his spot again, leaning against the marble counter near the big sink. He stared at Jack over the rim of his coffee mug.

"So you don't think she's attractive?" Liam challenged, changing the subject from Jack's supposed misdeeds.

"I didn't say that." And he wouldn't. Because she did have some very appealing attributes.

"But you don't think we have a chance with her. So, is the fact that the two of you got off on the wrong foot just an excuse? Or do you really not like her?"

"Maybe we did get off on the wrong foot. Mostly because she's a lunatic."

"She's not a lunatic." Liam's voice was curt. That got Jack's attention quickly. Liam was the most laidback person he'd ever met, but this morning, he'd been on the warpath.

This was far more serious than Jack had first thought.

"Look, you're right," he said, keeping his tone gentle. Which was not easy right now. "I shouldn't have said that. I shouldn't judge her for her car either." He tried out a grin. "Although in most states, that car could serve as legal proof of the state of her sanity."

That was supposed to be a joke.

Liam was very much not laughing.

Shit.

"All right. I'm sorry. I'll behave from now on. With you. And with her."

"What does that mean?"

"What do you think? If you really have your heart set on her, let's give it a shot. I'm willing to put in a few dates, see how things go. I want you to be happy."

Liam nodded and then took two big steps across the kitchen to where Jack was sitting on a stool at the island. He dragged Jack into a kiss. A surprisingly passionate one.

It was a kiss that had him wanting to lure Liam back into the bedroom and then getting naked and fucking like wild men.

But he had work to do. He had to meet with one of the contractors later this morning. He had a state inspector who was looking to get his sign off on paperwork. He didn't have time to indulge in any early morning naughtiness. As much as he regretted it.

Liam drew back from the kiss. He smiled that sweet Liam smile and leaned his forehead against Jack's, looking into his eyes.

"That's all I ask. A chance. I know you two will love each other if you get to know each other."

"Whoa. The word 'love' is off-limits. For now,

anyway. I'll be happy if she doesn't try and run me over next time she sees me."

"I think she'll surprise you, Jack."

He shrugged, happy that Liam was happy, but still holding some reservations. Liam was wild, free, very chill, and a bit naïve, if truth be told. He was at least a quarter modern-day California hippie—in spirit at least. Liam didn't really give a damn about money, or having a lot of it, but he certainly liked to give it away. Jack actually admired that about him. He didn't have a bunch of sexual hang-ups either, which was why he'd been the one to encourage Jack into their first ménage relationship. A relationship that Jack still looked back fondly on. Liam believed that someday the world would truly celebrate love over hate and prejudice instead of only giving lip service to the concept.

Like Jack had said: naïve.

Jack was far more cynical, he hated to admit. That was one of the reasons this Lighthouse project was so important to him. He'd watched as good jobs left his hometown, his home state, moved off-shore by big corporations who didn't care about little town main streets or average people. He was willing to put his money where his mouth was too. And sometimes, playing in this world meant acting like a dick.

But he trusted Liam. And he loved Liam more than anything. He sure as hell didn't want to lose him over this...or anything else. He knew that wasn't really something he should fear. Liam had always been devoted to him, and Jack felt the same. But part of him, the more cynical, glass-is-half-empty part of him, worried about it anyway. He couldn't imagine a future without Liam.

So if Liam believed this woman might be something special, Jack needed to get his head out of his ass and really give her a chance. He couldn't sabotage this by acting like a bastard. That would hurt Liam. It would lower Liam's opinion of him. And he'd already had all of that he could stomach this morning with their almost-fight.

"I'm going to go see her today," Liam told him, grinning again. It was so easy to make the man happy that he wondered why he didn't do it all the time, every second of every day. Liam's grin made him feel like the king of the world whenever he saw it. "To her cookie shop. As cover, I'll need to buy plenty of her stock of fresh-baked cookies."

Jack laughed. "You sure you aren't just interested in her because of your obsession with cookies? You hate cake. You hate candy. But this woman must seem like an angel from heaven with her cookies."

"A man thinks with two things," Liam announced. "His stomach, and his cock."

"But not his brain, apparently."

"Brains are overrated. So, are you coming?" Liam waggled his eyebrows. "I'll buy you a cookie."

"I would, but I can't. I have meetings lined up with contractors and inspectors, remember?"

"You can't reschedule?"

"Not these. But look, you should probably go solo to avoid me accidentally scaring her off. The whole, three-people-fucking-each-other element can blow people's minds, and not always in a good way. And we both know she isn't too keen on me. Yet." He shrugged. "This way, you can put in a few good words for me."

God knew he would need it.

"You aren't completely behind the eight ball. Rebecca complimented you on how well you spoke to the city council. So you should take that to heart. Also, no one fell asleep when you were talking. Another tally for your win column."

"Thanks...I think." But he was inexplicably pleased that she had complimented him to Liam. Maybe she didn't completely hate him.

Maybe this crazy idea had a chance after all.

Or maybe he was just as naïve as Liam was.

He suspected that soon he would find out.

That didn't mean he wasn't worried. As he got ready to leave for the day's work, his worries settled in as if they meant to stay.

If this somehow went wrong, would it finally be the thing that drove a wedge between the two of them? He prayed he would never find out.

And as happy-go-lucky as Liam was, he hoped the man he loved knew what he was doing...

CHAPTER FIVE

Rebecca

Tuesdays were slow. Summer tourist traffic was lower on a Tuesday. Most visitors left town either Sunday or Monday morning at the latest, heading back to their homes and jobs and lives.

It was two in the afternoon, another low ebb for Cookie Nookie business. In the early mornings, she was busy making fresh cookies for the shop and for delivery. Then from nine until ten, she made daily deliveries around town to the handful of restaurants that used her cookies as part of their dessert menus, or she headed to one of the local coffee shops. On certain days of the week, she hit the other tourist and antique shops that sold Cookie Nookie cookies from the cash register counters or in little displays along with other local favorites like fudge and jellies.

After her deliveries were made, she opened the shop. People would swing in after lunch for cookies and coffee. Nothing fancy. Some people would come by after work. But the afternoon was usually empty. She mostly used the time to pick and pack any online orders or to make cookie cakes for parties and the like.

But today, she had no orders to fill, either online or for parties. She'd already cleaned and wiped everything down twice. Now she was sitting behind the cash register, reading a book on her smartphone. It was a Highlander romance. Full of kilts and sexy accents. Yum.

The bell over her front door jingled. Rebecca looked up, excited about a customer.

It was Liam Collins.

He was dressed in cargo shorts, a blue T-shirt, and an unbuttoned, short-sleeved shirt. She knew he was supposed to be rich, but right now he looked like a man in his late twenties, maybe early thirties, ready to play volleyball on the beach.

She liked that about him. True, he looked jaw-droppingly gorgeous in the designer suit she'd seen him wearing at the trade show. But he also looked so...normal and down to Earth and yet still jaw-droppingly handsome in casual clothes.

She gave him a great big smile and put her phone down. "Welcome to Cookie Nookie. A piece of cookie heaven."

He grinned right back. "That has to be true, because I am a man in heaven right now. I do love me some cookies. Jack says I have an addiction, but I swear I can quit any time." He tilted his head to the side a little, looking at her with his longish, dirty-blond hair dangling across his forehead. The look in his eyes was warm but focused.

That look made her feel like maybe cookies weren't the only thing on his mind.

She felt her heart race and tried to cover up feeling flustered by looking out the windows behind Liam and asking, "Where's your significant other?"

"Jack had meetings. And more meetings. So I'm on my own." He walked along the glass display cases. "I have to admit something. Remember the box of your cookies I bought at the trade show? I ate that in one afternoon. Now I'm jonesing for more. What do you recommend?"

"Honestly, I hate to toot my own horn, but they really are all delicious. Do you have any nut allergies?"

"Nope."

"Then you can't go wrong, even randomly picking. Or you could get another box. Or two. I stand by my product, one-hundred percent."

"I like that. Okay, right now I'm going to go with a peanut butter cookie and the classic chocolate chip."

"Good choices." Rebecca put on plastic gloves and took a clean set of tongs to grab the cookies he wanted from the display case. She put them in wax paper and handed them over. She couldn't deny how eager she was to impress him. This was something she did best, serving customers and making people happy with her baking, so she really did want to make a great impression. It helped her confidence that he'd already liked the samples and cookies he'd bought at the trade show. With a small business like hers, word of mouth was very important.

He took a bite of the chocolate chip cookie. It was a bit of a cliché that women were always the expressive ones when it came to delighting in food. Liam had no qualms about proving that wrong. His lips wrapped around the top of the cookie, and he again let out an almost sexual groan of pleasure as he took a bite and chewed. His eyes even rolled up in his head for a moment.

A thought hit her like a thunderbolt. Was that what he looked like when he was making love with Jack? Did he make those delicious sounds when Jack's mouth was on his cock?

She felt herself starting to get hot and wet, her pussy suddenly clenching with need. She wondered what it would be like to kiss Liam. To run her hands through that thick hair. To have him making the same erotic sounds because of something she was doing to him.

Quickly, before her brain could break even worse than it already had, she shoved those thoughts away.

"That...was so good," Liam said, wiping away crumbs from his lips. The chocolate chip cookie was gone. "I only meant to take one bite, but once I started, I couldn't stop." He held up his remaining cookies and glanced at the three small tables in the front of her shop. "But I have more left. Care to join me? Or is that not allowed since you're on duty?"

"I think I can get away with it," she replied. "Since I'm in tight with the boss."

He laughed. She felt like she'd just won some kind of triathlon or something by making him laugh and seeing the way his eyes lit up. How weird was that? And yet, she couldn't deny it. His laughter, and knowing she was the one to make him laugh, made her all warm inside like fresh-baked cookie dough.

"Can I buy you a cookie?" he asked. "I'm willing to share mine, but the more cookies, the merrier."

"I wish all my customers said that. But no, thank you. I get enough of them." She patted her hips a little self-consciously. "I'll let you in on a secret if you promise not to repeat it. Cookies might taste like they're from heaven, but they are the devil for your backside."

"Please. You look great."

A blush burned on her skin, as hot as a sunburn and probably just as red. He'd said that so quickly, as if he didn't even need to think about it.

As if he believed it.

"T-that's kind of you to say," she managed to stammer.

"Kind? No. True? Yes." He walked to one of the tables and put his cookies down. He waited for her to join him and held out her chair for her.

Once he was seated, he began to eat the other cookie. His eyes widened at the first bite, but she was disappointed she didn't get any more groans of pleasure. She suspected she'd be replaying that sound and his expression in her head later when she had a little girl-time with her vibrator.

"Now, one last thing," he said as he finished scarfing down the last cookie. The man did not mess around when it came to eating. "I'm going to need to buy a few boxes of cookies. I'm thinking five to start, but I could go as high as ten. I need to make sure Jack gets his own box so I don't need to share." He grinned and winked at her.

She didn't know what to say. If he bought that many, this would be Cookie Nookie's best business day in a week.

But she was still hesitant. Was this some kind of way he was trying to make up for Lighthouse? Did he feel guilty about reassuring her that Lighthouse wouldn't put her out of business? She'd admitted that she was afraid of exactly that.

Oh God, why had she ever admitted that aloud? And to a man who was romantically involved with the owner of the company that might bankrupt her? Was she insane?

She really needed to learn to keep her big mouth shut.

But either way, she was going to take his business and fill his order. He could guilt-buy all the cookies he desired.

"I can do five boxes or ten, whatever you'd like," she said. Hoping, of course, that he bought ten.

"Ten it is! You talked me into it." His eyes twinkled with amusement and made her pussy clench again. She was so slippery down there right now, all because of this man and his damn ultra-sexiness and those groans that seemed to vibrate right through her body to her core.

She got ahold of herself and scolded herself to focus on reality, not some foolish fantasy. What was next? Would she be imagining Liam in a kilt and melting her with a delightful Scottish accent?

"I'll get it ready," she said, starting to rise from her chair and trying not to drool over Liam in a kilt.

He caught her wrist though, stopping her. He didn't hold her hard. In fact, his grip was very tender, even if she could tell how powerful he was. He was watching her with those unforgettable eyes.

"Before you go to put together my order, I wanted to ask you something."

Uh-oh. Was he going to ask to buy her recipes like Jack had? Or was this something to do with her spilling her guts and making a fool of herself last night? Or maybe he was going to ask her where she'd learned to drive.

She really hoped it was the last one. If he asked those other two, it was really going to break her heart.

"Yes?" she managed to say around a tongue that

suddenly felt too big for her mouth.

"I want to take you out to dinner. There's a good restaurant in Portland. I think you'd like it."

"Is that…is that why you ordered all the cookies?" It was the first thing that popped into her mind.

He looked confused, as if he had never even considered that. "What? No, not at all." He looked at her, and then he burst out laughing. "Why? Is that going to work? Because hell yeah, I'll order all the cookies you have if it means you'll say yes."

She stared at him, and then she realized she was smiling. It was impossible to be mad at this man. How could she say no to his offer of dinner when she had so much fun in his presence? Not to mention how he made her feel…

But there was one a huge, insurmountable problem.

"Wait. You're with Jack." She felt her expression avalanche its way into a scowl. "I won't cheat on anyone. That's not the kind of woman I am."

Then she felt her skin go hot again, this time with embarrassment. Had she read too much into his offer? Was this simply meant to be a dinner among friends and she'd overreacted? God, what must he think of her now?

But when she met his gaze, there was no laughter in Liam's eyes and no smile on his lips. He was very grave when he answered her. "I would never ask that of any woman, much less you. I love Jack with all my heart. For us, that goes without saying."

"I don't understand. Is this just a 'friend' thing?" Her neck felt like a branding iron pulled right out of the fire. She was making such a fool of herself.

Yet she felt powerless to stop.

"No," he said, staring right into her eyes. He didn't seem so laidback and easygoing now. He seemed like a wolf on the hunt.

And was she the prey?

Maybe. Either that or the cookies. It could go either way.

"No," he repeated, then sighed and leaned back in his chair. "It's definitely not a friend thing. It's time I was upfront about things. It's easier to understand each other if people just open up and talk, right?"

She nodded warily even though she wasn't

completely sold on that idea. Because every time she opened her own mouth, she shoved her foot right in it.

"I find you very attractive," he said, his charming grin nearly melting her from the inside. "I have since the moment I first laid eyes on you at the tradeshow. I liked how you handled yourself there. And I liked that you let me help you, even though you thought I was the enemy."

"Enemy? No, I think that's a bit of an exaggeration…"

Although, if she thought about it carefully, it probably wasn't much of an exaggeration. At the time she had been heated about Lighthouse Bakery. Upset and very worried. That didn't bring out the best in people.

Who cared about that now, though? Because had she misheard, or had this gorgeous man with the billion-dollar smile really just told her that he found her *attractive*? Was this a dream? Had she found a magical genie in some lamp?

No, she definitely didn't remember rubbing any lamp. The only thing she enthusiastically rubbed these days was her clit, precisely because she didn't have a good man in her life and no good prospects on the horizon. Of course, she would go to her grave never having admitted aloud what she'd rather crudely thought just now.

But...was that all about to change?

She couldn't believe it. Was he going to leave Jack Meacham for her?

He shrugged after considering what she'd just said. Words she couldn't even remember now. Something about enemies, maybe? All she could think of was this man and her pussy, and maybe getting them together and how glorious that would be.

"Okay, not an enemy," Liam said. "But I was smitten, I admit it. I looked up your business online while we were at the tradeshow. I was planning on coming in to see for myself, and then lo and behold, we met in the parking lot at city hall. As if fate intervened."

Fate was an asshole if that was how fate chose to intervene. She would have nightmares about hitting Mercedes Benzes for the rest of her life. But that wasn't the point. The point was that this man was already involved with someone else.

"Jack..." she said, almost plaintively. Trying to

get her tongue to obey her. It didn't want to. It wanted to believe that this man really liked her. She couldn't blame it. Not at all. "You... He..."

"Jack is bisexual, the same as me. I might have told you that." He rubbed his chin, leaning back, looking as if he was judging something tricky. Like jumping across a hundred-foot-wide canyon. "We've had ménage relationships in the past. Several. It's always us and a special lady we care about."

Her eyes went wide. She might have sucked in a breath in surprise. Then she scolded herself. It wasn't as if she was the ultimate prude. But acting as if this had been Victorian times and she was packed in a corset and ready to faint in outrage...that was just plain silly.

Besides, she was intrigued.

Also...how hot was that? Two gorgeous guys banging each other and with a woman occasionally sandwiched in there too? That was a lot of cock to have to handle. Would she even be up to it?

Yes. Yes, she would.

And finally, Liam Collins thought she was attractive and (if he was mentioning ménages) he wanted to screw her. With his lover. Both of them drop-dead gorgeous (even if one of them was an arrogant jerk). Should she be flattered? Was it wrong to say that she was?

Of course…there was still Jack Meacham. Did he want this? Last time she checked, he was no fan of hers. And he definitely wasn't on her Christmas cookie list right now.

But maybe that could change?

"You're very quiet," Liam said, watching her closely. She got the sense that he wasn't new to this exactly, but that he might be a little nervous. Or at least concerned. He seemed so invested in her answer that she had to take a deep breath and really think. She didn't want something foolish to pop out of her mouth. God knew half the thoughts in her brain were broken right now.

"It's a lot to swallow," she said. "Or, I mean, a lot to take in."

She blushed. That was an innocent statement— there was nothing wrong with the word "swallow"— but her horny brain kept assuring her it had to do with blowjobs. Namely, Liam filling her mouth with hot cum and her swallowing it down—

All right. Enough. Until further notice, her brain and all her fantasies were on total lockdown.

He ran a hand through his hair, artfully disheveling it. She couldn't believe he could get away with messing up his own hair and still look good. Some people had all the luck.

"It *is* a lot to take in," he said. "But I've found it's usually good to be blunt and upfront about things. That way, there are no misunderstandings. Yes, what we have is not a common thing, I realize that. Some people would be offended by its very existence. I respect that—it's not for everyone—but I'm hoping you're not one of them."

"I'm not easily offended. Honestly, I'm more curious than anything. And flattered, of course. What woman wouldn't be? But honestly…Jack and I don't really get along. So where would that leave things?"

He grinned. "Jack has put his worst foot forward twice in a row with you. But he is a great guy once you get to know him. Kind and generous and fun. He's very special to me, and I have great taste. But I'm also looking for someone to share him with. Another special someone."

She stared at him, not knowing how to respond. Part of her was enthusiastically saying *YES!* But she wasn't some kind of wild college girl. Well, not anymore. There were too many problems with this. For example, she wouldn't have the first idea what to do in a ménage. The simple answer was: get fucked by two guys. But how did it all go down? Who did whom first? Were there rules? It was intimidating.

Also, she shouldn't be thinking about the sex more than what an actual relationship with them would be like. How did loving two other people work, exactly? Was there jealousy? Did two guys mean that the toilet seat was always left up? What was the reality?

Most of all, as attracted to Liam as she was…she was still uncertain about Jack Meacham. She'd freely admit that the man was very handsome. But she feared they'd be at each other's throats all the time. The big billionaire investor with his fancy industrial bakery versus the plucky heroine who sold cookies to tourists. That kind of thing didn't have a happy ending in real life.

"Listen, Liam…" She took a deep breath, trying

to think of how to say all of that to him.

He smiled, but it wasn't a happy smile. "That's not a good sign. A big pause followed by the word 'listen?' It means I'm going down in flames, doesn't it?"

"Like I said, I *am* flattered. I…I can't believe I'm saying this, but I really don't think it would work out. I mean, you love Jack. That's wonderful, but I would only be getting in the way."

"I understand why you would think that," he said. "But in a good ménage relationship, each partner helps deepen the love and the relationship between *all* three. No one gets in the way. Of course, there are challenges. There always are. But it doesn't hurt to come with Jack and me on a dinner date and stick a toe in the water. There's a five-star place in Portland that has great seafood. We would love to take you there. Nothing else. I know I threw in the word ménage right away, and everyone only thinks of the sex, but we would never pressure you into anything you didn't want or weren't ready for." He took her hand and looked deep into her eyes. "You have my promise on that."

"You both want to take me out to dinner?" she

asked, wanting to go...and knowing it wasn't a good idea. She tried to laugh, but it came out a bit choked. "Does Jack know about any of this? I mean, he seems more the arm-candy supermodel type."

He tilted his head and eyed her, for the first time seeming a bit...what? Disappointed? Maybe disappointed in her?

"I'm going to just say that you don't know him very well," Liam said. "Yet. Give him a chance." Now his smile came back, brilliant as ever. "Give *me* a chance to take you out and show you a good time."

Hell yes, she wanted that. More than anything. Well, almost anything. She still had her self-respect. And if Liam loved Jack, and Jack maybe hated her because she'd rammed the back-end of his Mercedes, then this whole thing was dead from the get-go. Besides, she was beginning to doubt herself. What could a man like Liam or even Jack see in her? She was not beautiful. She was not rich or powerful or famous. She was nobody.

She stood and quickly pushed in her chair. Her throat was tight with emotion. Not good emotion either. She felt like she was seconds away from crying.

But since she'd already done that once and embarrassed herself completely, she was determined not to do it again.

Why had he come here? Did he believe she would fall all over herself for a chance at them? Well, he was wrong.

"I should get back to work. I'm very busy," she said, hoping he wouldn't remember that she'd been reading on her phone when he'd come through the door. "Thank you for the dinner offer, but I just don't think it's a good idea."

She walked back around the counter. She put a smile on her face as if none of this mattered. As if she hadn't just told a handsome and rich heartthrob that she didn't want him to take her to dinner at a fancy restaurant. She was crazy. This proved it.

And yet, this was better than going and having Jack ruin her night, and then her life, by putting her out of business when his fancy factory opened and he betrayed her for profits. At least her heart would be safe.

Lonely, but safe.

Liam stood, put his napkin in the trash, and then

turned to her. He didn't come close, didn't crowd her.

"I appreciate you hearing me out," he said. "I'm disappointed, but I respect your decision. If you don't mind, I'd like to still swing in and buy some cookies from time to time." He leaned toward her conspiratorially. "Because just between you, me, and the wall, your cookies are way better than anything I've tasted from Lighthouse Bakery."

"Oh! Um, of course!" She couldn't say no to that. She *wanted* to see him, even if it might be difficult. She liked being around him, liked the way he made her feel, loved those smiles. She only hoped things wouldn't be awkward...but he'd taken it all in such stride that she didn't think it would be awkward. Not on his end anyway.

He said goodbye and left. She admired his butt in blue jeans as he walked out. She couldn't help it. Part of her was afraid that, despite his words, this would be the last time she ever saw him. Especially with Lighthouse opening up in a month or so. Jack would probably make him stop coming to see her. That arrogant jerk.

Although, now that she thought about it, Liam

didn't seem to be the kind of man who would be told what to do by anyone. He was laidback, sure, but he wasn't beta in any sense of the word. She couldn't help wondering how the relationship between the two men went. What happened when they argued? Did they end up wrestling until one of them was victorious?

Because she'd pay to see that, she thought with a grin.

But now that her shop was quiet and empty, she began to second-guess herself. Had she made a stupid, terrible mistake? It had all happened so fast...and now that Liam was gone, she was beginning to think that she had made a mistake. Maybe she had been a coward and was missing out on something unforgettable.

No. She had to think of her business first. It was important to her. There was no way anything could work out between her and Jack. Her and Liam... Her cheeks heated and her pussy clenched just at the thought. Although Jack Meacham was handsome and debonair and all of that, he was still an arrogant, brutish jerk who had made her cry and tried to steal her recipes.

Maybe that didn't really make sense in a strictly

"true" sort of way, but that was how she felt right now.

With a sigh, she took to her stool behind the register again. Hopefully, things would pick up when people got off work and came in for cookie cakes and desserts for parties and such. Until then, she would have to distract herself by reading.

Highlanders might be the only way she could keep herself distracted and not worry about how she might've just made the biggest mistake of her life.

CHAPTER SIX

Jack

Two days later...

J ack stood outside the small Cookie Nookie storefront. The place was smaller than he'd expected. It really was crammed between a solid-looking bank and a post office straight out of the forties. Now that he was here, he could see why she'd gone with the play on the word "nook."

The shop was cute. It had curb appeal, despite being tiny. The awning was red. The front window had bright white decals with a bold font, easy to see from the street. *Cookie Nookie. Delicious cookies inside! Come on in!*

He stood on the sidewalk with his hands shoved in the pockets of his suit trousers. Not going inside. Not leaving.

Why was he here? She didn't want to see him. He'd already rubbed her the wrong way. More than once. He'd burned all the bridges.

Oh, yes. That's right. He was here because of Liam.

He sighed, running a hand through his short hair. Liam didn't know he was here...but here he was.

All right, so he admired this Rebecca Johnson. A little bit at least. Well, more than that. There had been a very good reason he'd offered to buy one of her cookie recipes. It was that damn good. It certainly had Liam hooked, and Liam should know. The man was some kind of cookie junkie.

But yes, Jack admired her because she was a small business owner. The backbone of America. He simply admired her...what? Gumption? Drive? Her dedication in showing up at the tradeshow? Even though it annoyed him, he respected her for not putting up with his shit. For being insulted when he tried to buy her recipe...even though he wished she'd given in on that one. He could make millions selling that cookie to a broader audience statewide. Maybe even nationwide.

Screw it. Time to head inside. He was only wasting time out here.

It was late afternoon. He'd just come from a meeting with the lead contractor that had ended early. He'd decided to come here to see what he could do to set this right. He had taken it as a personal affront that Rebecca had turned Liam down.

Liam wasn't pouting about it. Liam didn't pout. Still, it was clear he was disappointed. Two days ago, he'd he told Jack about coming here and inviting her out to dinner with the two of them...and dropping the whole bisexual ménage stuff on her. He'd had to keep himself from rolling his eyes. Liam liked to be direct, straightforward, open. Usually it worked for him, along with his charm. This time it hadn't...and Jack had a feeling that he was the cause.

So he was here to try and make things right.

Somehow. If he could.

If it worked, he would let Liam know she'd agreed to go on a date with them. If it didn't, he'd keep his failure to himself. Even being successful might irritate Liam. His lover was big on letting people find their own path, not leaning on people or pressuring them.

That was all fine and good, but if you wanted results, sometimes you had to make a good case. Sometimes you had to fight for them.

Besides, what woman ever knew what she wanted? They spent hours looking at shoes. Then they had buyer's remorse.

All right, *maybe* that was a rather unfair stereotype. And probably a lazy and insulting way to think. Liam would probably kick his ass if he'd said it out loud.

Anyway, he should probably get this over with before he had any more second thoughts.

Jack opened the door and stepped inside the shop. A little bell over the door jingled. The bell was a nice touch.

Rebecca was helping a customer at the counter,

ringing up an order. She caught sight of him, and her smile froze on her face. Her eyes flashed, but she turned back to her customer, handing back the change with a renewed smile. The customer took her order and walked out, leaving them alone together in the small shop.

"I like the bell," he said, trying to break the ice. "Very homey. Small town and all that."

She glared at him. "Is that an insult?"

"No. Not at all." What was it with this woman and her prickly nature? Or at least she was certainly prickly when it came to him. "I admire it. It reminds me of growing up." He shrugged. "I wish there were more places like this still around."

She eyed him suspiciously as if judging whether or not he was lying to her. "We're a dying breed. It's all big box stores now."

That was a thorny thing to talk about. Especially since she might turn her ire on him for some reason he couldn't yet fathom.

He decided it was best to be frank with her. He didn't have the patience for games right now. "I'd like to talk to you if you have a moment."

"Are you here to 'buy' another of my recipes?"

"Ah, no," he replied, rubbing his chin. "That was a mistake. Not that I wouldn't love to buy that recipe if you're selling, but I realize now that I might have come off as too aggressive."

Liam had let him know—in great detail—why he'd been acting like an ass when he'd offered to buy her cookie recipe.

She frowned at him. "I'm surprised you'd admit to a mistake. I expected...different."

Score one for him. Now all he had to do was not act like an ass and piss her off again. So far, that had been easier said than done.

"I'm full of surprises," he said, risking a smile.

She didn't smile back. "Buy a cookie."

"I'm sorry, what?"

"If you want to stay here, buy a cookie."

"Fair enough. What do you recommend?"

"That's like asking me to choose a favorite between children. I love them all."

His eyes widened in surprise. "You have children?"

She rolled her eyes. "No. But if I did, it would be

the same. Get it?"

"If you say so. How about…molasses."

"Good choice." She put on food-handler gloves and used tongs to take a cookie from the plate in the display case and put it in a wax paper wrapper. She handed it to him.

He paid for the cookie with cash and took a bite. Just the right amount of chewiness, rich molasses flavor, hints of ginger and cinnamon, but not too sugary.

"This is really good," he said. "Do you make these from scratch?"

She nodded. "Usually every morning. So, now that you've had your cookie, why are you here? You said you wanted to talk. So talk."

He appreciated that she got right to the point. He didn't want to have to spend half his life talking around the issue. "Liam told you about us."

"He did."

"He asked you out on a date."

"Right again."

"You said no."

"You're batting a thousand." Her eyes

narrowed. "Did you come here so I can tell you 'no' as well?"

She was certainly spicy when she got her fur up. No wonder Liam liked her. Jack wasn't pleased she was raking him over the coals like this, but at least she wasn't one of those suck-up, toadying people who only pretended to like him because of his money. When her eyes were flashing like that, and she had her head tilted, glaring at him, she was quite striking.

"Not exactly. I wanted to know if you turned Liam down because of me."

"Yes. Now buy another cookie for the road and please tell Liam 'hi' from me."

He couldn't help it. She'd surprised a laugh out of him. "You don't pull any punches, do you?"

She sighed. "Look, Jack. I don't punch anybody at all. Ever. I'm nothing but a cuddly teddy bear. But I really don't know why you're here. I think it's more than just asking me if I turned down a date because of you."

"I'll tell you why if you'll tell me why you hate my guts."

Her eyes softened. She looked away, shaking her

head a little. "I don't hate you. Not really. I don't hate anybody."

"I do seem to rub you the wrong way, though. I don't think you can deny that."

"I did...um, crash into the back of your car. So I'm sure I'm not your favorite person either."

He shrugged. "At the end of the day, it's just a car. Nobody got hurt. That's what counts." Liam had made that abundantly clear to him too. And he'd been right. Jack had plenty of money to deal with any damages.

She nodded, her brow creased...and maybe it was his own elevated self-esteem talking, but he got the feeling she had warmed to him. A little bit.

Rebecca seemed to make up her mind about something. "Okay, if you really want to know, I'll tell you why you're not my favorite person in the world right now."

He put his hands in his pockets and rocked on his heels, waiting for her to go on. After a moment, she did.

"Because I'm a small business. A tiny one. What happens to me when your big industrial bakery takes over everything? You can price me right out of business, and you know it. This shop is everything I have. I don't want to lose it."

He frowned. "Don't be absurd. You're not going to lose anything."

"Absurd? Excuse me? *I'm* being absurd when a huge competitor shows up in my town and starts throwing money around? That shouldn't make me nervous? I know everyone's excited about the jobs. I'm happy for them. I know I'm the outlier. What I don't get is why you don't understand that."

He frowned, thinking about what she'd said, looking at it from her point of view. The point of view of a small business owner who depended on her business *staying* in business and how his arrival could make her feel threatened. Maybe he'd been an ass for simply assuming she'd see things his way. He knew she didn't need to be worried. Well, nothing was for certain, but he'd tasted her cookies, and they were damn good.

A place making cookies this good should never go out of business. If anything, she needed to work on marketing and expand her customer base. But he bit his tongue from telling her that. For once, he had enough foresight to guess how his advice would sound to her. He didn't want to piss her off any more than he already had.

Liam would be proud.

"I'm telling you, I'm not here to drive you out of business. That isn't even remotely the plan."

Her little store wasn't big enough to warrant anything like that. But again, he bit his tongue, knowing saying that wouldn't go over well.

"So you say." She leaned forward over the counter a little, her eyes flashing. "I could easily end up collateral damage. And you already tried to buy one of my recipes out from under me. What am I supposed to think?"

"What will it take to convince you?"

"More than inviting me out to dinner, that's for sure," she snapped.

It struck him right then. She wasn't simply cute. When her eyes were full of fire, with her chin tilted defiantly, she was beautiful. And it was damn annoying. First, because it was distracting him right now. Second, because *he* was the person she was defying. Why the hell would he think she was beautiful when she was being an obstinate pain in his ass? This woman was trouble. That was all there was to it.

After he realized both of those things, it was her lips that caused all the trouble. He made the mistake of glancing at them. They were full, lush, and so very kissable. Her lips were parted slightly and close, since she was leaning toward him.

Before his brain could lodge a protest or convince him this was insane, he leaned forward and kissed her. Her lips were just as soft and warm as he'd imagined. His cock immediately began to stiffen in his pants, letting him know exactly how much it approved of this development.

He felt and heard her indrawn gasp of air. Now that he was touching her, he was helpless to do anything but deepen the kiss as passion rose inside him. It was mixed with frustration, desire, and a need to make her understand. To prove something to her.

For a wonderful moment, she didn't pull away. She let him kiss her.

Until she didn't.

She put a hand on his chest and pushed while

drawing away at the same time. After she was free, she stood there with her eyes wide. Her hand came up, and she touched her lips.

He had to swallow a groan. Her finger against those full lips made the ache down in his groin intensify into something so powerful it was almost painful. Her light brown eyes stared at him. He stared back at her. The flash of passion and fire that had been in those big brown eyes while she had argued with him was gone.

Now there was something else. Surprise, yes. Or maybe shock was a better word. But something else too. Desire? Or was he merely projecting?

"Why did you do that?" she asked. Her voice was strangely calm. As if she were asking why he'd left an umbrella out on the porch.

Was she going to make him explain? He'd been suppressing any and all attraction to her because he knew she would be a pain in his ass and cause nothing but trouble.

And look at that. He was right.

Those feelings, those urges he'd kept clamped down had suddenly shot to the surface. If she wanted proof of his attraction to her, she had it. But now he had to deal with the fallout of his actions, good or bad.

He glanced at his imaginary poker hand of responses and decided to go all-in with confidence. "Because you were beautiful. Because it suddenly seemed like the only thing I could do to convince you that I'm no threat to you. Exactly the opposite, actually."

"And you think it's okay to show that with a kiss?" she asked. But her voice was soft, and her eyes weren't angry. "I should slap you. But I'm not the kind of person who hits."

His mouth curled into a half-smile. "That's good. I'm not the kind of person who likes to get hit."

"Was that a joke?"

God, he was crashing and burning all over the place. He *never* crashed and burned with men or women. He was practically Don Juan. Only Liam had ever stolen his heart for long. But this woman...she had thrown him completely off his game.

He'd come here to invite her to dinner. For Liam's sake. Because Liam liked her.

Then he'd ended up kissing her. And right now,

his cock was harder than iron, making it difficult to think. How had he made such a mess of this?

She was watching him with those pretty eyes, waiting for an answer.

Go with the truth then. "I was trying to make you smile with a joke, yes." He shoved his hands in his pockets and let out a long breath. "Look, you're pretty, damn it. I don't blame Liam for being interested. He thinks he can be respectful and persistent and get you to change your mind about coming on a date with us. I think you've made up your mind. But I had to try."

"So you tried to convince me..." she said. A smile with the slightest hint of wickedness about it lingered on her lips. "With non-verbal communication?"

She meant the kiss. Clever. He found himself grinning, liking her even more. This woman was a pain in his ass for all kinds of reasons. One of which was the fact that she'd rammed his car and then made him feel ten tons of guilt about it when she started crying about it. Oh, and not to mention driving him to kiss her—which had been a shock to them both.

"When I try, I like to go big." He dropped the

smile, turning serious. "Will you let us take you out to dinner? Nothing more than that. I know this is a lot to take in, but Liam is the best man I've ever met, hands down. He likes you. He wants to get to know you better."

And apparently, so did Jack. Especially if the unexpected kiss and the raging hard-on were any indication. That kiss had been a huge risk. It might have been a mistake, but if it actually got her to agree, it would be worth it a thousand times over.

Besides, he'd really enjoyed tasting those warm, soft lips of hers.

He already wanted to do it again.

"One date?" she said, eyeing him as if she half believed it was some kind of trap.

He raised his hand as if swearing an oath. "One date. If you enjoy it, then maybe you consider another. If not, you can have fun telling me to hit the road. Promise."

He could see that she was thinking it over carefully. Then she got that defiant look again. "I'm not sleeping with both of you on the first date. If that's why you're here, don't waste my time."

Jake ran a hand through his hair. Damn, just the thought of her naked and between silk sheets was making his cock nearly bust its way out of his pants. "I promise. I won't even try and kiss you."

"Your track record on that is a little spotty," she quipped, eyeing him.

He couldn't help a smile because she wasn't cursing him or throwing things. Was he winning her over? Maybe he still had it after all.

"A good point," he said. "But Liam will keep me in line. He's my better half."

"Yes," she said, narrowing her eyes. "I can see that."

He cleared his throat. She had agreed with that sentiment rather quickly. Well, since she was agreeing, he hoped it was getting to be a habit. Time to put all the cards on the table and win the game.

"So, will you come to dinner with us this Friday? I know Liam wants to take you to a place in Portland that's unforgettable. Best seafood in the city."

"Let me check my calendar." She picked up her phone and idly swiped the screen, double-tapping apps or whatever.

She was clearly making him wait. She wanted to see if he was patient.

He could play this game like a pro. He simply watched and waited, making sure his expression told her exactly what he *wanted*.

She shook her head. "Okay, fine. I'll go. I have to admit...I'm curious." Her stare was probing, intense. It actually made him a little uneasy, as if he didn't have as much control over the situation as he'd assumed. "But if this is what the two of you want—God knows why—then I'm willing to take a chance. For Liam. I'm still not convinced you won't put me out of business, but I'll be honest. If Liam loves you, and you're kissing me, then maybe I should take a chance."

"That's music to my ears. You won't regret it, Rebecca."

"I'm sure I probably will. But that's never stopped me before."

He liked the sound of that. Damn, Liam was going to flip when Jack told him that he'd managed to convince her to give them a chance. It made him feel good, really good, to do things for Liam. To make him happy. He always felt complete, like a whole person when he made Liam smile or brightened his day.

Of course, he had to admit that he was curious too. That kiss... Well, it had sent shockwaves through him. The only other person who made him feel like that was when he kissed Liam.

He held her gaze. "Thank you," he said, meaning it. "For giving this a chance."

She nodded, biting her lip. On a whim, he bought a box of cookies for Liam (which made her smile) and said his goodbyes.

After climbing behind the wheel of his car, he simply sat there for a second, stunned.

What the hell was he doing? Kissing *this* woman? The female convinced he was twirling a mustache and trying to drive her cute little store out of business?

Hell if he knew. But he had cookies and good news for Liam, and life had just gotten a whole lot more interesting for them all.

CHAPTER SEVEN

Liam

They left to pick Rebecca up at her apartment that Friday. Liam was usually pretty easygoing, but he'd been excited all week. Tonight he was doubly excited. They had rented a limo and a driver from New York. The limousine was a white stretch with all the trimmings and high-tech bells and whistles. Even though the Benz's damaged back-end had been repaired, they both agreed they wanted the extra room a limo provided, along with the ease having a chauffeur drive them around the city.

And, of course, to impress Rebecca. That most of all.

Besides impressing her, Liam didn't want to take a chance that the Benz would bring back bad memories for her. He wanted tonight to be fun and exciting for her. She'd taken a chance with them after all. He wanted to make certain she didn't regret it for an instant.

"You nervous?" Jack asked him gently as they rode in the back of the limo, just entering Fremont now. A huge bouquet of roses sat on the seat near him.

For most of the ride, Liam had been quiet, caught up in his own thoughts. Not something usual for him. He was an extrovert. It was no wonder Jack was asking him that question.

"To be honest, I am." He chuckled and shook his head. "I don't think I've been nervous about anything since my first 'date' date with you."

Jack was grinning at him. "You were nervous back then? That's adorable. It didn't show."

Liam eyed him. "Yeah. Weren't you nervous? A little bit?"

"No." Jack's gaze intensified. "Because back then, I had a feeling we belonged together. I knew you would be mine."

"I don't know whether to think that's confidence or arrogance."

"Both."

He snorted. "Well, as for me, I was nervous because I wanted you in my life so badly. I don't usually want things."

"I know. You're the least material-world person I've ever met. And I love you for it. You help keep me in check."

He smiled, warming at the compliment. "Yeah, but the downside is that when I *do* finally want something, I can't always maintain a Zen attitude. That's how I felt about you...and it's how I feel about her."

Jack's expression shadowed a little. "Liam... I don't want to see you hurt. I mean, I want her too. I want her with us. But most of the time, these things don't work out. I may have stunned her with my kiss—God knows I stunned myself with it—but she might be having second thoughts. She already turned us down once already."

"You do realize that as a cheerleader or support coach, you really kinda suck right now."

Jack chuckled softly. "You're right. I just want you to be happy."

"I know."

"And I shouldn't have kissed her first. It should have been you. You saw her first."

Liam waved that away. "Come on. It's always been *us*. We don't compete with each other. If that kiss convinced her you weren't the jerk she thought you were, then I have no regrets."

"Good. I think."

"Yeah, it's good. But if she had slapped you for being so forward, you would've deserved it."

He rubbed his chin, his expression rueful. "True. I usually don't lose control like that. She just looked so..." He shook his head.

"What? Don't keep me in suspense."

"Beautiful. Defiant. Fierce. It was like I meant to use all of these arguments to convince her to take a chance on us, and they all went flying out the window when I got close to her. I had to take that last risk and gamble everything."

"I know. There's something special about her." He frowned, picturing her heart-shaped face, those lush lips, dark lashes, and her high cheekbones. Something about her appealed to him in a way all those fashion models or centerfolds never could. There was something real to her. A down-to-Earth beauty. Not a wholesomeness—not exactly. But a warmness, a realness that he missed whenever he was in a big city like New York among the rich and powerful.

Hell, maybe he should have kissed her back at the tradeshow when the thought had first rocketed into his head. Was being so easygoing actually hurting his game? But after a millisecond of considering, he dismissed the idea. It had been a trade show, for God's sake. They'd just met. If he'd tried that kind of intimacy right off the bat, he would've deserved a knee in the balls. Jack had taken a risk by kissing her, but he'd done it as a last resort. Like he'd said, it had been a final gamble.

Jack was watching him closely as if reading his thoughts. "There is something about her," he said. "So it's time for me to tell the truth and shame the devil.

I'm nervous too. I wasn't nervous back when the two of us were starting out, but with her..." He shook his head again.

Liam knew what he meant. "With her, it's definitely not a sure thing."

"Exactly. She's a wild card. And that fascinates me."

"But we can do this. And I believe she's worth it."

"I think so too."

A few minutes later, they arrived at her apartment complex. The siding was red, the roof and trim painted black. The place looked tired, a bit rundown. They could hear someone playing bass-heavy music that thumped through the air. The apartment complex reminded him of a place he'd lived with his mom when he'd been in middle school. People struggling to get by, doing their best.

Maybe that was why he felt the sudden urge to tell Rebecca he would pay to put her up in a better place, renting a house even. He wanted her to be safe and happy.

Hold your horses, hombre, he warned himself. *Let's*

finish a first date before you decide to tell her where she should be living.

Good advice. He couldn't just go all alpha on her. She would tell him to take a hike. And she'd be perfectly justified in doing so. He didn't know where this side of him was coming from. It didn't fit with the mildly annoying nickname Jack sometimes used for him when he was irritated that Liam wasn't riled up about something that really didn't matter. Laidback Liam. He would have to be careful.

They left the chauffeur with the limo, took the roses, and headed to her apartment on the second floor. She answered the door right away. His breath caught in his throat as soon as he saw her, and for a moment, he was speechless.

She looked absolutely stunning.

She wore a burgundy, v-neck cocktail dress that came just below the knee. The dress had straps, not sleeves, and it had cascading ruffles that managed to look elegant without hiding too much of her body's curves. The v-neck was just low enough to show some cleavage, straddling the line between sexy and tasteful. She wore simple black strap heels, and he did love a woman in heels.

As they stared at her, she smiled at them tentatively.

If she hadn't won his heart already, that tentative, hopeful-but-a-little-nervous smile would have clinched it for sure.

"You are beautiful," he said, handing her the roses they'd brought.

Her eyes widened. "For me? Thank you!" She brought the flowers to her nose, smelled them, and sighed. "They even have a scent."

Jack raised his eyebrows. "Do roses not have a scent anymore? When did that happen?"

Liam threw a sidelong look his way. "Some of them don't because they've been genetically modified over time, bred for how they look instead of how they smell." He glanced at her again. "Please excuse Jack. He's an ignorant heathen. Clearly, he has little experience buying people flowers."

She grinned. "All right. I'll forgive him. Just this once."

Jack made a show of bowing. "My lady, I am in your debt."

That made her giggle. Liam felt a surge of hope, maybe even joy, at the sound. It told him they might have a chance at this after all. He knew he was supposed to be the calm and carefree one, but here he was, reacting like a guy who managed to get a pretty girl to go with him to the prom.

He must really and truly have it bad for her. That, in itself, was a sign.

After she put the roses in a vase, they escorted her to the limo.

Her eyes widened when she saw it. "Is that yours, or did you rent it?" She stopped, seemed to realize what she'd said, and winced. "I'm sorry. That was such a rude question."

"No worries," Liam said. "Jack rented it for tonight."

"It's a company in New York I use all the time," Jack added. "Five-star service."

"I've never ridden in one." Rebecca raised her eyebrows. "So you'll need to be patient as I push all the buttons to find out what they do."

That made Liam laugh. No wonder they got along. The first time he'd been in a limo, he'd done exactly the same thing.

The chauffeur held the door for them. Rebecca made sure to thank him, and the driver beamed and tipped his hat to her.

Soon they were on the road, headed to Portland. Rebecca did indeed look everything in the back of the limo over and had fun pushing buttons and exploring, exclaiming over every amenity. Her enthusiasm had both of them grinning. It was good to have someone like her in their lives. Someone to remind them how damn lucky they were with everything they had. To make them humble and appreciate it. He opened a bottle of champagne and poured for the three of them.

"Mmm," she said after sipping the champagne. "Good. Do you think they'd notice if I stuffed a bottle of this down the front of my dress and ran off with it?"

"You don't have room for it," Jack said with a wicked grin, his gaze heated. "You fill that dress out perfectly."

Liam's breath caught as he watched for her reaction. That was Jack, weaving in a double entendre or two to let a person know he was interested. It had always turned Liam on. But personally, he might've held back on a comment so bold until later in the evening. Or at least until after a glass of champagne, when people were a bit more mellow.

Although Jack was right. With those gorgeous, full breasts, that delectable cleavage, and how tightly the dress wrapped her, she had no hope of hiding anything down the front of her dress.

He loved it.

Rebecca took the comment as the compliment it was meant to be. Her eyes twinkled as she glanced at each of them. "A girl isn't supposed to admit this aloud, but I'm glad someone noticed."

"Oh, we noticed," Liam said, his own voice rough with the surge of desire that had taken hold in him. It was raw and powerful. The force of it took him by surprise.

He'd always thought her attractive, with a low-key and warm sexiness that had caught his attention from the moment he'd first seen her. But now, seeing her in this dress that emphasized her curves, and catching the scent of her perfume, it stirred a primal part of him even more.

Liam wanted to touch her. To trace his fingers

along that soft, creamy skin. To feel her warmth. He wanted to kiss his way up her neck, breathing in her scent before claiming her lips as his own.

He wanted to watch as Jack did the same, the two of them driving her wild. Giving her the time of her life. Giving her the pleasure she deserved.

It was no surprise that his cock was as hard as steel now, aching as it throbbed in his suit trousers. That piece of him only ever had one thing on its mind. He needed to slow down. The sexual tension in the back of the limo was as steamy as a sauna right now, and from the way her pupils dilated, her lips parted, and from the directness of her stare, she was feeling it too.

Liam had gone into tonight with no expectation of getting laid. Tonight was all about romancing her. Showing her that two men were better than one—and not just in bed. Putting to rest as many of the fears that came along with a non-standard relationship as possible. And mostly, letting her see what a good man Jack was when he wasn't acting like an ass.

But now his body was quite clear in what it wanted. It wanted her. And Jack. Both of them.

Together. And he wanted them *now*.

Jack was the one to ease off. He leaned back in the big leather seat and glanced at Liam. "Liam picked the restaurant, and as usual, he made a great choice." He turned those blue eyes back to Rebecca. "I think you'll enjoy it."

"I'm sure I will. Do you both go there often?"

Jack shrugged. "We go to all kinds of places. Liam's always trying out new restaurants. Even greasy spoons and food trucks." He chuckled and threw Liam a fond look. "For someone who likes to wear 'comfy clothes' and eat macaroni and cheese fancied up with bacon and hot dogs, Liam does have *some* good taste."

Liam threw a sidelong glance Jack's way. He was going to pay for that one. So what if he liked board shorts and T-shirts, especially when out on the sand or the water? A man needed to cut loose and be easy sometimes. But the quip about macaroni and cheese and hot dogs was just low.

Rebecca was grinning. "Guys have it easy. Most of your outfits are comfortable, and you only have to worry about matching your tie. Even your shoes are comfortable. It's a man's world." She glanced at Liam, her tone still gently teasing. "If you can eat mac and cheese and hot dogs, I guess it would be easy to cook for you."

"All you'd need to do is feed him a few cookies from time to time," Jack added. "And you would win his heart forever."

She was still looking at Liam, her gaze direct, almost challenging. "Good to know."

Liam rubbed the back of his neck, shaking his head a little. How had this suddenly become all about him? "Look, I shouldn't have to justify my trashy tastes. I'm a well-rounded human."

"You like my cookies," Rebecca said. "So I think you have *excellent* taste."

"Thank you." He made a show of glaring at Jack, who looked endlessly amused with the trouble he'd caused. "And I'll have everyone know my love for mac and cheese with bacon and hot dogs comes from when I was growing up. My mom used to make it for me every Friday night."

"Aw. That's sweet," Rebecca said. She reached out and touched his wrist gently, leaning toward him a little.

He had to control himself and not admire her cleavage. Instead, he nodded, looking right at Jack with narrowed eyes and a tight smile on his face as if to say: *Yeah, that's right. She said it was sweet.*

Jack only grinned. *Score one for you,* that grin seemed to say.

Liam turned the conversation back to Rebecca, asking her about where she was originally from. The mention of the dish his mom used to make had resonated with him more strongly than it had in years. He'd been raised by a single mother. They hadn't had a lot of money. Adding bacon pieces to the dish had been his mother's big splurge because she knew he liked it. They used to sit in front of the TV and watch cartoons together.

Why was he getting all choked up about that? Was it because his mother had died almost a decade ago? She'd been a victim of cancer, and her loss had hit him hard. Was this some kind of weird thing where he thought his mother was a good, caring woman and he thought Rebecca might be the same—even though she looked completely different?

Slow down. Take it easy. You're thinking too much.

Psychoanalyzing things on a date was never a good sign. Especially when mother memories were involved. Usually, he was the epitome of easygoing and relaxed on dates. Even past threesome dates had never rattled him.

Why was this different? Was it because he wanted Rebecca so badly? Was the fear of not having her throwing him off his groove?

He didn't know. But he had to work to maintain his easy, even-keeled demeanor, and that was something new.

Even Jack even seemed to sense it. Jack covered for him nicely though, showing his charming side to Rebecca instead of the side he'd shown her so far. Which was the unsubtle, bull-in-the-china-shop Jack who'd insulted her by trying to buy her secret recipes and then made her cry after a traffic accident.

But she seemed to be keeping an open mind about Jack. That was good.

Soon they arrived at the restaurant near the waterfront in Portland. It was called Back Cove Steak and Seafood. They had a reservation for a private room. After they were seated and the sommelier had taken their wine order, they immediately eased back into their conversation. Rebecca was talking about her time at the New England Culinary Institute. Jack talked about growing up in Maine, something he had in common with Rebecca. Liam kept things going smoothly by making jokes and asking gentle questions designed to get her to open up. He found her fascinating. And so, it seemed, did Jack.

Rebecca ordered a stuffed salmon fillet with a crab leg appetizer. Jack had steak—a porterhouse, medium-rare. Liam had grilled swordfish and collards. The food was delicious. He could see it impressed Rebecca, and he was glad she was enjoying herself.

After the servers had cleared away their plates, they refilled their glasses with French wine, and an easy silence fell between the three of them. That was a big thing Liam always looked for. How comfortable were the silences? Did everybody rush to fill them? Were they awkward and aching, desperate for some kind of relief or a way to ease the tension? Or were they smooth and easy and comfortable?

He could only speak for himself, but these quiet stretches felt smooth and calm, almost restful. But he didn't feel the need to rush in with a joke or an interesting story. He was content to let those conversations and words happen as they may.

Rebecca didn't seem nervous either. No fidgeting, no strained smiles, no glancing at her cell phone for the time or playing on social media. That was a good sign. She listened, and she laughed, and she made her own jokes, told her own stories. Like the time a pregnant woman chased her cookie car into a parking lot, desperate to buy some cookies. The woman threw a twenty at her, grabbed a box of oatmeal raisin cookies, and thanked her while waddling away at high speed. Well, pregnant-lady high speed.

In other words, Rebecca certainly wasn't boring.

She leaned her elbows on the table, resting her chin on her hands. "The meal was amazing," she said with a contented sigh. "Better than Fish Taco Friday down at Luis's Grill."

Jack had been taking a sip of his wine and suddenly choked on it.

Liam broke out in laughter. Grinning, he glanced at Jack. "You going to survive? Maybe long enough to come with us to Fish Taco Friday?"

After wiping his mouth with a napkin, Jack chuckled and shook his head. "I'm fine. You just surprised me into simultaneously laughing and swallowing. But I'm sure Fish Taco Friday is memorable. We'll go there next week."

"No, no, that's okay," she said quickly. "I'm not sure fish tacos would hold up against what I just ate. I'm ruined for life." She smiled and sipped her wine. "Thank you for the wonderful meal and the amazing company. I hope I'm not gushing, but I had a great time."

"Gush away," Jack assured her. "My ego is insatiable."

Liam grinned. "He's not lying either. But I hope you aren't ready to head home yet. We have a limo. The night is young. The town is ours."

"Ooh," she said. "I like the sound of that."

"What would you like to do?" Jack asked. "Dancing? Maybe a club? Drinks? Or we could go walking out on the town. Maybe the waterfront?"

"Definitely the waterfront. I haven't been there in a year, but it's one of my favorite places."

"The waterfront it is."

Liam did his best to hide the surge of relief he felt when she agreed. He'd thought the night was going surprisingly well, and he was having a great time, but he definitely wasn't ready for the evening to end. A glance at Jack showed him that they were on the same page. Jack was at his most charming and friendly—and it was genuine too. Jack wasn't a man who faked anything. He was either all-in, or he didn't even play.

It was such a relief that the two of them were getting along so well. He wouldn't lie. One of the reasons he'd been nervous was because they'd gotten off to such a rocky start. But they had certainly clicked tonight. He had to admire Rebecca for even giving Jack a chance, taking a risk, jumping into something so new it must feel very strange to her.

Liam couldn't deny the sexual tension in the air either. Every smile, every glance, only kept that sexual tension and desire simmering. And damn, did Rebecca ever look beautiful. She was stunning, the soft light making her skin glow and her pretty eyes shine. Just glancing at her lips made him ache to kiss her...and had him shifting in his seat to relieve some of the growing pressure in his groin.

He wasn't going to push things, sexual tension or not. He was going to lay back and let whatever magic happened, happen. He would count the night a win just to see her smile.

Of course, it would be a double win if he managed to score a goodnight kiss.

More than that only seemed wishful thinking, no matter how much chemistry the three of them had. It almost seemed greedy to want more...even though he did.

Liam took a sip of his wine, stealing another glance at her. This was only the first step on a long journey to winning her heart. *That* was what he wanted.

She caught his glance and smiled. He smiled back.

Time to start earning what he wanted.

CHAPTER EIGHT

Rebecca

The limo dropped them off at the waterfront. Rebecca had always loved coming down here, even as a kid. Her father used to take her from time to time. They would watch the ships, watch the fishermen, watch the gulls and the waves.

Tonight, it was foggy. Liam had asked if she wanted to call it off and go somewhere else because of the fog, but she said no. Sometimes she liked the fog. It made things mysterious. It changed up what you were used to seeing. She knew that was weird because usually people only liked sunny, beautiful days. But ever since she was a kid, there had been something fascinating about the fog.

Tendrils of mist wrapped around the pier and the railings as the three of them walked the waterfront. The lights were dull, glowing orbs overhead, their illumination not reaching far. It was very quiet, almost muffled. She could hear the foghorns. She could hear the nearby traffic, but because of the fog, it sounded dim and far away.

But even though it was quiet, peaceful, her body and brain hummed with excitement. Had her heart ever slowed down from its rapid beat all night? No, she didn't think it had. This seemed like some kind of fairy-tale night with two Prince Charmings. She didn't want it to end, even if that did sound greedy. Being this close to them really got her blood rushing through her veins. Seriously, she had to keep herself from drooling over them. And when they looked at each other with love in their eyes, sharing a moment or a laugh, it made her knees weak to see.

So what if she harbored a secret fantasy that

someday they both would look at her that same way? She was only human. A girl could dream, couldn't she?

Tonight she'd been assailed by fantasies ever since she'd opened the door to see Jack and Liam waiting on the landing outside her apartment. From that instant on, her heart had been in her throat. They had looked so yumilicious in those suits and brightly colored ties. When they smiled at her, she practically melted like butter in a hot pan.

Her ego was sitting pretty too. When they first laid eyes on her all dressed in her best (and sexiest), she noticed their eyes widening as they took her in. She'd spent almost an hour on her makeup. She'd had an emergency session with her hairdresser. Now she looked the best she could look. Their reaction—the interest, the heat, the *desire* in their eyes—wasn't hidden from her. It sent a lightning bolt thrill zapping through her.

Oh, and it also sent a bolt of pure lust rocketing straight for her pussy. What woman didn't want to be looked at like that? As if she was the most beautiful, important, desirable being on the planet. She loved being looked at that way. Well, she loved having Liam and Jack look at her that way.

She struggled to push those thoughts to the back of her mind. She was getting turned-on again, and it was distracting.

Now the three of them were walking along the waterfront together, but after all the great conversation at dinner, no one was talking much now. No one seemed to feel the need to break the quiet. She was walking in the middle between them, with an arm hooked through each of their arms. They turned off the main street along the waterfront, down one of the long wharves. Their footsteps echoed on the wood of a long pier. Many of the warehouses, shipping containers, and restaurants were shrouded with fog.

"I came here quite a few times as a kid," Jack said, breaking the stillness. His voice was soft, lost in memory.

She glanced at him. "So did I. My dad used to take me here for ice cream and to see the ships and the fishermen. I loved it. I used to watch the seagulls and pretend I could fly."

Liam was grinning at her. He had a warm charm to him, but his smile always dazzled her. "I bet you were a cute kid."

"I was an awkward kid," she said, shaking her head. "A late bloomer."

"You're beautiful now," Jack said.

The way he said it—so matter-of-fact—made her believe him. Or at least believe that he felt that way and was telling the truth. She warned herself that she was susceptible to flattery and then ignored the warning. Right now she was feeling too good for warnings.

"Jack's right," Liam said, his voice low but fervent. His charming smile had gone, and his eyes were uncharacteristically intense. "And I dare anyone to say different."

She felt her cheeks and her neck flush with heat. She opened her mouth to protest...and then stopped herself. Why should she be self-effacing? If they wanted to tell her how they thought she was beautiful, then she wanted to hear it. Their words made her chest clench, and her throat tighten with emotion.

They made her feel *good*.

Still, all she could do was give them a shy smile, not knowing what to say. Having these men want her, having them talk to her as if what she had to say really mattered, treating her like…like a princess, was heady. It went to her head faster than any amount of wine, leaving her almost dizzy. It had her turned-on, her blood racing, her pussy wet.

All week she'd been afraid of fighting with Jack on this date, that things would go horribly, that she'd made a mistake agreeing, especially after that…after that kiss. She had considered calling up and canceling a dozen times. Her desire to see Liam again had stopped her.

But tonight, Jack had been a completely opposite human instead of a human-shaped jackass like he'd been before. He was funny, charming, warm…and sexy as hell. Now she was afraid that he was simply a master of seduction, using his masculine wiles on her.

But that kiss… She had felt the passion, the desire in it. That kiss had lured her in. Or at least convinced her to give him a chance.

Right now, she was happy. She was horny. She didn't want to even blink because she wanted to remember every instant that happened tonight. It had been such a wonderful time.

"I don't want this night to end," she admitted,

speaking so low that she was almost talking to herself. "It's been magical."

"We have the limo all night," Liam assured her. "We could drive all over Maine if you'd like."

"Don't tempt me," she said, laughing.

Both men seemed to like it when she laughed. She wasn't certain if it was the sound, the positive feedback, or how she'd been told that her eyes warmed up and shone whenever she laughed. Or (since they were guys) maybe she was reading it completely wrong. Maybe certain parts of her anatomy jiggled when she laughed and it was as simple as that.

Whatever it was, she liked to laugh. It was definitely better than the alternative. So this was working out nicely.

Right now, the night was calm, maybe a little eerie with the fog, but beautiful in a strange way. The foghorns were a melancholy sound. And so was the slap and slosh of water against the columns of the pier. But she felt happy. Happy to be here with them…and excited too. Because she couldn't deny the building sexual tension between them. It had been ramping up from the moment she'd opened the door and seen them looking so gorgeous standing there on her doorstep.

She didn't have the strength to fight it. Her mind could warn her body all day long that putting out on a first date was not the kind of behavior a lady indulged in. But her body only said *to hell with that* and wanted what it wanted. Her pussy was ready to get fucked, hard and fast and for as long as she could take. It was a primal urge, something raw and intense. She was fighting to keep that urge in check. The fact that they were so near, touching her even, was not helping.

But she wasn't going to let them go either.

After reaching the end of the pier, they moved to the rail, standing very close to each other. They were looking out over the dark, fog-shrouded water and the piers and boats all docked for the night.

"I love being around places like this," Liam said, his voice gentle with musing. "Around boats, around the water. I'm glad both of you like it as well."

"We go sailing a lot," Jack told her. "Liam has a sailing yacht. I might have mentioned that already. It's a lot of work, but as he likes to say, it keeps us in shape. Do you like to sail?"

"I've only been out on a sailboat once. I didn't

have a lot of opportunity for that kind of thing when I was growing up. I do love the ocean, which is why I couldn't live in the middle of the country. I'd feel lost without some kind of ocean nearby."

"I feel exactly the same way," Liam told her.

She glanced at him and put her hand on his upper arm. Yes, she was very aware of how tight with muscle his upper arms were. If he didn't work out with weights, then sailing really did keep you in good shape.

"Have you been sailing ever since you were young?" she asked, having difficulty keeping focused on her words and not his biceps.

"No. I came into it late." He shrugged. "My big thing was surfing and body-surfing in high school. But my college roommate's family had a decent-sized sailboat. He used to invite me to go sailing with them all the time. That's where I learned."

"That sounds wonderful."

"It was. He's still a good friend. The first thing I did after selling my app for a ridiculous amount of money was buy them a new sailboat. They had to sell theirs to help pay some health care costs."

"You paid their health care costs too, didn't

you?" Jack said gently. "That's what I remember."

Liam shrugged, suddenly seeming uncomfortable. "It's not fair for a family to have health insurance and still lose everything to bankruptcy paying for cancer treatments the insurance won't completely cover." He shook his head and took a deep breath, letting it out slowly. "Sorry. This is a touchy subject for me."

Jack was staring at Liam fondly, his eyes filled with love. "He doesn't like attention or praise for helping people," Jack said softly to her. He suddenly turned his gaze and met her eyes, his stare almost challenging. "Tell me, how can a guy like me not fall for a guy like him?"

How indeed?

These men could not be real. They were too perfect. Or maybe Jack wasn't, despite how perfectly charming and friendly he'd been tonight. She wasn't going to forget how the two of them had clashed, even if she could forgive it and even if she was willing to give him a second chance. A chance to prove his promises about not driving her out of business were true. But Liam was some kind of national treasure. It reassured her that a guy like Liam could love a man like Jack Meacham. It meant that Jack was worth the risk. Or at least, that's what she wanted it to mean.

It scared her how much she suddenly wanted both of them in her life...as friends at the very least.

No. She shouldn't lie. She could easily imagine them as lovers. Nothing else would be good enough. She had never been involved in a ménage. It wasn't even one of her fantasies...until now. Now, it very much was. But man on man? That was a fantasy she'd had for a very long time. Two guys going at it with all the intensity, all the pure, raw lust that men brought to the table? Oh yeah.

She shifted on her feet a little, her pussy now dripping wet. She needed to get a hold of herself and control of her thoughts. Now here she was, all wet and ready to go, thinking about men fucking each other.

But...was that wrong? She had a hard time convincing herself that it was.

She was done playing hard to get...if she'd ever even started. If these two amazing men played their cards right, they could have anything they wanted. And she would love every second of giving it to them.

"—to go sailing with us sometime?" Jack was asking her.

Rebecca tore her distracted thoughts away from sexy times and tried to focus on what he was saying. "I'm sorry. What was that?"

"Would you like to go sailing with us sometime?" Jack repeated. "Jack's the outdoors type, way more so than me, but I have to admit, I always feel better after spending some time with him out on the water." He was watching her closely. "It's perfectly safe. He's a very good sailor." Now he gave her a grin. "He keeps me right in line."

"I'd love to," she said. "But you probably shouldn't let me anywhere near the wheel. I'd hate to crash into something."

That earned her a laugh from both men, and she was glad no one was holding any grudges about her little accident.

"That's a lot harder to do out on the open ocean," Liam said. "You'll enjoy it. I can teach you anything you'd like to know."

They talked a little more, making plans for a day's sailing on Sunday when her shop was closed.

After that, they were quiet for a time, watching the night and the drifting fog, feeling comfortable with each other.

Finally, she glanced at them, her curiosity getting the better of her. "How did the two of you meet?" She hesitated. "If you don't mind my asking."

"Not at all," Jack said. "We went to the same university. Boston University, actually."

Her eyes widened. "You've been together since then?"

"No, no," Liam said quickly. "We were only acquaintances back then. He was in the business program. I was in software engineering. We used to carpool to hockey games."

"After we graduated," Jack continued. "We went our separate ways. But we met up again in New York. At some kind of charity event. I don't remember what it was exactly." He glanced at Liam. "Something to do with the environment?"

"It was a clean seas charity. To deal with plastic and garbage in the ocean."

Jack smirked. "Yeah, I should've guessed. But when I saw him again, I knew." He shrugged. "It was a love-at-first-sight-only-not-really kind of thing."

"What does that mean?" she asked.

"Because we had known each other before, so I guess it doesn't count as love at first sight. But when I saw him again, I knew he had to be mine."

"It sort of counts," she said. "When you saw each other again, things just finally set, like concrete."

"Something certainly went hard." Jack's grin was wicked.

She burst out laughing along with Liam.

"After that, we started dating," Liam continued. As if by some unspoken agreement, the three of them began to walk along the waterfront again, heading back the way they'd come. "That was years ago."

"And..." She hesitated, wondering if the question she was about to ask was too probing. Then she said *to hell with it* and asked anyway. She really wanted to know. "You're both bisexual? So there were...women?"

Neither man seemed offended by the question. Jack looked at her frankly. "Sometimes. It was always us, but sometimes we let other people into our lives."

"I believe in sharing our love," Liam said. "With

the right people. We had a few good relationships that lasted. For a while, anyway. But these kinds of relationships have their own challenges."

"And their own rewards," Jack finished.

"You guys should sell timeshares," she said, giggling. "I'm already convinced."

She realized what she'd said and bit her lower lip, wondering if she'd blurted out too much. So much for being demure. Maybe she could blame the wine.

"Good," Jack said, his eyes intense as he looked at her. "Because not just anybody catches our eye. Hell, I don't care if I sound arrogant or selfish, but not everybody's worthy of sharing with Liam."

Liam stopped, and she stopped with him. He had his arm on hers, and he was looking her right in the eyes. "He means that it takes a very special person to hold our attention. Someone kind and honest, who knows how to laugh, knows how to live."

"All of that," Jack said, "But he forgot to add 'sexy and gorgeous.' Because we *are* men, after all."

She didn't know what to say. Her skin felt hot, like she was standing under a heat lamp. Her chest felt tight. Her breathing had quickened.

It turned out that she didn't need to say a word. Liam drew her into his arms, and she went willingly into his embrace.

His kiss left her head spinning, her heart pounding even faster. She was practically clutching at him to keep herself steady. His arms around her were so strong. She didn't want him to let her go.

"I don't want this night to end," she whispered for the second time that night.

If they didn't catch the clue and take her somewhere private where they could make crazy love to each other, then they were as dense as badly made pound cake.

It turned out they weren't dense. Their eyes told her everything. They were watching her with such heat that she was nearly melting right there.

"Liam," Jack said, his voice rough with desire. "You heard the lady. Let's take her home."

CHAPTER NINE

Jack

The limo dropped the three of them off at Jack and Liam's house in an upscale east end neighborhood of Portland. They'd bought the place a year and a half ago when he'd first put in motion plans for Lighthouse Bakery. He'd paid an interior decorator to fully furnish it so he didn't have to be bothered. The house was only two million—the smallest, oldest, and least expensive one he owned. But Rebecca was impressed anyway, even though he could tell she was trying not to be.

That amused him, and it made him like her even more. Hell, the lust was there. She looked as if she'd been poured into that dress, and she was all curves and beauty, and he swore he could still taste her on his lip from that surprise kiss in her shop. Watching Liam kiss her had been one hell of a turn-on too. But it only made him more eager to get his hands on them both.

So the sexual energy, the tension was present in spades. But she was also adorable. It was very clear to him now what Liam had first seen in her. He was glad he had the chance to pull his head out of his ass and see it too.

She was very real. That was an odd thing to say, but it felt right too. She wasn't any New York socialite or any gold-digger looking for a payday. She was impressed with the house because she lived in an apartment and worked hard to pay her bills. If anything, it made him more appreciative of what all his wealth gave him. He and Liam both donated a lot to charities and causes, but it was easy to take things for granted. For example, thinking of this house as "only two million." That was the epitome of taking things for granted.

He was only glad he hadn't said that out loud. He wanted to show off what they had, but he sure as hell didn't want to make her feel poor or unsuccessful. He also didn't want her thinking he was shallow and greedy, concerned only with conspicuous consumption, overpriced cars, overpriced houses, overpriced wines, and overpriced everything.

"Shall we head inside?" Jack asked, raising a hand toward the big double front doors.

"I can't wait," Rebecca said, her eyes still wide as she looked the house over. "I bet this place has a great kitchen."

"You're talking to the wrong man," Liam said with a chuckle. "Jack can find the fridge, and that's about it. But it is a good kitchen."

She took their arms, walking between them again as they escorted her up the wide front steps. Touching her sent a thrill racing through his body. Her closeness made him ache to touch her more.

The ride from the waterfront back to the house had been a wonderful kind of torment. The expectations of what was coming sizzled in the air.

There were little touches, lots of smiles, light conversation, but all three of them knew and anticipated what was to come. Women were harder to read than men, but he could tell by her body language, her warm eyes, her parted lips, the way her gaze tracked them, and how she responded to even casual touches that she was just as into this as they were.

Jack had to force himself not to tell the limo driver to start speeding. He wanted to get them both naked. And he wanted to get them in bed.

It would be the perfect end to a perfect night.

That was the romantic way of looking at it.

But there was more to that truth. If he were completely honest, he had to admit that he really, really wanted to fuck them both. At the same time. The three of them together. He wanted to claim them both, to fill them, to make them his.

He wanted to taste Liam's lips, to kiss the hell out of him, to hear him groan with pleasure.

And Rebecca. He wanted to drive her wild. He wanted to leave her satisfied and breathless, to rock her to her core and have her wanting even more. He wanted to hear her moans, her bliss, to revel in her pleasure.

Just thinking about it had his cock hard and throbbing. That ache in his groin was a distraction, his need driving him on. Since it was clear the three of them wanted the same thing, he would do everything in his power to give both the man he loved and this new, amazing woman the time of their lives.

Then he would do the same tomorrow morning.

And then tomorrow night.

He unlocked the front doors with a biometric key. Fancy, fancy. He'd had all the tech in the house updated to the newest gadgets on the market. Liam told him he was ruining a Victorian, but Liam was secretly just as much of a gadget lover as he was.

Liam took the opportunity to pull Rebecca into his arms and give her a long, lingering kiss. She wrapped her arms around him, pressing tightly against him. Jack moved up behind her and lowered his lips to the creamy bare skin of her neck. He took in her scent, an alluring perfume mixed with a scent all her own.

She arched for him as he kissed the sensitive skin on her neck and behind her ear, nibbling playfully at the seashell curve of her ear. He ran his hands along her sides, from her hips upward.

When Liam broke the kiss for a moment, Rebecca was left breathing fast. She put her little clutch down on the foyer table and then she ran a hand through Liam's dirty blonde hair as Liam switched places with him. Now Liam was kissing along her neck, and Jack got a chance to turn her head to him and capture those tasty lips of hers.

The kiss was easy to get lost in. He could kiss her for days. She was so responsive, so curvy and firm in all the right places, that she had him achingly hard already. She could feel his erection, and he almost groaned when one of her hands dropped down and skimmed over where it pressed against his pants. She smiled against his lips.

"I'm guessing we're going to skip the kitchen tour," Liam murmured playfully as he paused from kissing his way down her neck to her chest, and the bit of exposed cleavage the v-neck dress revealed.

"Tomorrow," Rebecca said breathlessly, her eyes half-lidded with lust. She looked so sensuous and beautiful that he had a hard time not stripping her right there and fucking her up against the front door. "All I want now is the bedroom tour."

"The best room in the house," Jack said, his voice roughened with his own need. He loved how forward she could be. She knew what she wanted and didn't hesitate to tell them.

They led her through the house to the second floor where the master suite was. It was slow going because they kept stopping to kiss, to caress, to touch and tease. It was a kind of stop-and-start foreplay that had him going wild. He and Liam had already left behind their suit jackets and ties and dress shoes, discarded as they moved and undressed. She had both heels off and the zipper halfway down on the back of her cocktail dress.

When they were in the bedroom, things got really hot, really fast. Rebecca stepped free of them for a moment, turned to face them both with a seductive smile on those perfect lips. Her eyes were so big, so beautiful and burning with her desire that he nearly fell to his knees to worship her.

As they watched, she slowly skinned the dress down her body, revealing lacy black panties and a strapless bra.

They both stood there admiring the sensual sight, reveling in it. Then, by some unspoken agreement, they both pounced. They swept her up in their embrace, Liam claiming her lips while Jack lavished attention on the rest of her body. He stroked along the inside of her thigh, teasing ever so slightly against the silk-covered heat of her pussy. He skimmed a finger across her nipple, delighting at the shudder and breathy sigh the touch drew from her.

Rebecca pressed herself closer as Jack caressed her breasts. He undid her bra hooks and freed her breasts. Liam drew back enough to admire them, taking them both and cupping them in his hands. Her large breasts were tipped with wide, dark nipples. He found them mouth-wateringly sexy. She moaned when he leaned in and his lips found her nipple. He sucked the hard tip and then teased it with his tongue.

"Oh," she sighed. "That's good."

He loved the pleasure vibrating in her voice. Liam continued to ravish her mouth. Jack moved positions for a better view. He watched as Liam slid his hand up her thigh, nudging her legs wider. He ran his fingers through her trimmed pubic hair, caressing her mons, then sliding his fingers over her slit. Jack watched, his cock throbbing, as her head lolled back in pleasure. Everything about her, about the two of them, was stunning. Their passion was stirring him even more. He watched as Liam kissed along her neck and slipped one finger past her pussy lips, slick with excitement.

He couldn't stay away for long. He moved to her side, turning her so that he could claim those lips and kiss her deeply.

Gently, he moved her so she could lie back on the bed. She went eagerly. Liam hooked his fingers around her panties and slid them down her legs, then tossed them over his shoulder with a wicked grin.

Jack moved in on him as she watched. With expert fingers, he unbuttoned Liam's shirt and let it drop to the floor, revealing the man's tanned, magnificent chest. Liam returned the favor, stripping off Jack's shirt and even sparing some attention to licking and grazing his teeth gently over Jack's nipples, stirring another groan from him.

Rebecca was watching raptly as Jack took the lead again, undoing Liam's belt buckle, pant's button, and unzipping him. Liam's thick cock practically jumped into his hand as Jack freed it. With a grin, he began to stroke it, paying Liam back for driving him wild seconds ago. He loved the way Liam looked when he was being pleasured, the way he reveled in it with complete abandon.

But it wasn't long before Liam was undoing Jack's belt and sliding his pants to the floor. Jack was achingly hard, his cock thrusting outward and upward, the slit already wet. Jack pulled Liam into a fierce kiss. They kissed naked, grinding their bodies together, reveling in the wonderful friction.

"Oh God," Rebecca whispered. "I could watch that all day."

Grinning, they turned their attention back to her where she lay upon the bed. Liam moved to her with languid grace. Her eyes widened and locked on his hard cock, bobbing as he moved.

Then Liam spread her legs wide and went down on her. Jack groaned as he watched Liam's tongue explore her folds. Her eyes rolled up, and she sagged back on the bed, sexy little whimpers and moans drifting from her kiss-swollen lips as Liam pleasured her.

Jack couldn't take any more. His lust was burning through his body. Quickly, he grabbed a condom and lube from the nightstand. He knew Liam's body extremely well. Liam was bent forward between Rebecca's legs, his bare ass in a perfectly tempting position. So it was nothing at all for Jack to coat his fingers with lube and teasingly work it along Liam's crack, down around his hole, then carefully inside, letting Liam's body adjust to the invasion.

Liam groaned as he continued to lick and suck Rebecca's pussy. Jack could see the top half of Rebecca as she quivered there, helpless under the attentions of Liam's skilled tongue. God, it was a beautiful sight.

He quickly slid on a condom and lubed himself up. Then he moved behind Liam, grabbed the base of his cock, and lined the tip up with Liam's hole. Liam shifted a little, encouraging him as he pressed forward with steady force. Then he was past the muscle and inside Liam's warm sheath.

Slowly, he thrust all the way forward, burying himself balls-deep in the man he loved.

And then he began to fuck Liam with deep,

steady strokes as Liam continued to enthusiastically eat out Rebecca's pussy so well he had her moaning and thrashing.

Liam was so tight, it always took Jack's breath away. It was always a struggle to keep from coming too soon when Liam's tight muscle was gripping his cock like this. Even with the lube, the pressure, the friction was maddening, pushing him toward the edge with each stroke.

He gripped Liam's ass hard, his fingers digging into the firm flesh. Now Rebecca was watching him from where she lay on her back. Her eyes were half-closed with pleasure, but she was still drinking in both the sight of Liam eating her out and Jack behind him, fucking him for all he was worth. Rocking him forward with every thrust, pushing Liam's tongue deeper inside her.

But Liam's tongue was dangerously skilled. Jack knew that very well. Rebecca was squirming now, her hips lifting and grinding against him as he teased her clit and then slipped his tongue into her channel before returning to her nub. Jack watched as she rushed toward an orgasm even as he fought to contain his own.

She let out a shuddering moan, her hands clenching in Liam's hair. She tensed, breathing fast. Jack watched her, knowing she was about to come. The sight was so damn sexy that he felt himself approaching the edge fast, despite his struggle to hold back and enjoy this for as long as possible.

"Wait, wait," she managed to say, utterly breathless. "If you keep that up, I'm going to come."

At her words, Jack slowed his strokes, fighting back from the edge. He'd almost lost it right then, coming too soon. But Liam felt too good. It always undid him.

Liam raised his head from her pussy. Jack couldn't see his face from behind like this, but he could imagine Liam's lips glistening with her juices as he smiled at her and said, "That's the idea, beautiful."

She still held his head, clutching him with both hands. Her eyes were closed, and she was breathing fast. Slowly, she shook her head. "No. I want you both. In me."

He stopped thrusting into Liam because if he didn't, he was going to blow his load for sure. Besides, now he had a new mission. Obeying Rebecca's demand.

Damn, this woman was something special. She wanted to go straight for the gold. He loved that.

Slowly, he drew back from Liam's ass. He reached down and grabbed the bottom ring of the condom, making sure it stayed on him with how tightly Liam was clenched down on his cock.

When he was out, he stepped back, his cock thrusting upward, long and hard and throbbing in outrage because he'd stopped before reaching his climax. His cock was greedy, but he was focused on giving Liam and especially Rebecca a good time. He peeled off the condom and tossed it in the wastebasket

Liam pushed himself up from between her legs. Jack ran his hands down Liam's back, down the V-shape of his back muscles. Then he pulled Liam around, dragging him into a deep kiss. They pressed against each other, cock to cock, and he pumped his hips a little, grinding against his cock, pleasure coursing through him.

He ended the kiss quickly, both of them turning to look at Rebecca, the one they both wanted to please the most.

She sat up and wiggled to the edge of the bed, watching them with wide eyes. He nearly came just looking at her, naked, her cheeks and chest flushed with pleasure, and those pretty eyes so filled with lust that she looked almost dazed.

"Just give us a second, gorgeous," he told her.

She nodded, her gaze sliding down their bodies to focus on their erections. That did all kinds of things for his ego, and he loved it.

Reluctantly stepping away, he took another condom and this time he rolled it down Liam's cock with slow, even strokes. Liam stood there, muscles rigid with the sensations of Jack stroking his cock.

As soon as the condom was on Liam, Jack quickly ripped open another and rolled it down his own shaft, giving himself a couple of good pumps, from the head down to his balls, just for Rebecca's sake as she watched their every move with such intensity.

He was smiling as he picked up the lube again and coated his cock, then coated Liam too. She was sopping wet from Liam's tongue in her pussy, he was sure, but he wasn't taking any chances. He wanted them both to be able to fuck her hard and fast, and the only friction he wanted was what finally drove her over the edge.

As for him, if he was going to take her luscious ass, he certainly had to be careful and take his time.

Liam turned to Rebecca, reaching out, taking her hand, and pulling her to her feet. He drew her against him, kissing her deeply, one hand cradling the back of her head, his other hand caressing one of her breasts.

While Liam had her distracted and consumed by the kiss and his caresses, Jack moved around behind her. He needed to prepare her too. But he didn't want to startle her. So he pushed her hair aside and started kissing his way down the curve of her spine. All the way down to the top curve of her ass cheeks. He kissed and bit at her—gently, of course—and he felt her responding.

He nudged her legs apart slightly, enough to give him access to her. He lubed his fingers, then with one hand, he grabbed her cheek and spread them. With his other, he teased around her puckered rear hole ever so gently, letting her get used to him.

He carefully coated her, letting her relax, letting

her adjust to him as he worked a lube-coated finger inside her. Then another.

She shivered with delight as he pierced her and made the sweetest, most erotic little moan.

When she was ready, Liam lifted her up. They were going to fuck her standing up, from the front and the back. It would be something she wasn't likely to forget any time soon.

Liam was gripping her ass cheeks, holding her up. Her legs were spread and wrapped around him, her arms looped around his neck as they both kissed deeply. Jack took Liam's cock and lined it up with her pussy, then guided her down on him. Liam impaled her slowly, and Rebecca quivered as he stretched and filled her.

Jack slipped back behind her again, grabbing his own wrapped-up cock with one hand. Because they were the same height, it worked, and they could balance her weight between them as they made love to her from two sides.

He dragged the tip of his cock from her taint up her crack and then down again as Liam fucked her pussy. She wiggled her ass, and he took that as encouragement, even though she could only make muffled sounds of pleasure against Liam's deep kisses.

That was all the prompting he needed. Slowly, his cock found her back hole, and he eased forward. She yielded to him, and after a moment he slipped past the tight muscle and buried himself inside her. God, her ass cheeks felt wonderful as he began to fuck her.

He lost track of time, falling into a haze of sensations as the two of them claimed her. With both of them in her, taking her at once, she did not last long. She began to tremble between them, shaking, and he felt her inner muscles clenched hard as an orgasm rocked her.

Now that she'd reached her climax, he knew he could finally let go and find his own.

He went rushing toward that breakpoint, all his pleasure peaking as the orgasm took him hard. His cock began to pulse, filling the condom with his cum as he buried himself inside her ass as deeply as he could. Waves of pleasure swept through him, the intense sensations in his cock rippling through him with every spurt of his cock. He groaned her name, helpless to stop it, dazed by the power of his orgasm.

Liam was not long either. He'd increased the pace of this thrusts, racing to finish with them. Jack had the pleasure of watching his lover's face, his head thrown back, his eyes closed, as he finally hit his own orgasm, tensed, and shattered into bliss.

For a short time after—how long, he couldn't have said—the three of them stood there, locked together so intimately, riding out the waves of their pleasure. Then, careful not to hurt her, Jack pulled out of her slowly, still supporting her. Liam did the same with equal care.

Afterward, they gently set her down again. She clutched at them for a moment, recovering from the intensity of her pleasure. They simply held her, all three of them breathing hard.

"That..." she gasped. "That was amazing..."

He nuzzled her neck, his erection finally gone, fucked into submission by the amazing sex they'd just had. "I couldn't have said it better myself."

Liam kissed her tenderly. "You're the amazing one, Rebecca." He glanced at Jack, love in his eyes. "And you too."

Jack leaned in to steal a kiss from Liam. He

could taste Rebecca on his lips, and that stirred his desire again, even after that knee-buckling orgasm.

These two were going to kill him. But he was going to enjoy every second of it. After that, the three of them curled up naked on the bed. He soon drifted to sleep, thinking happily of how perfect the night had been.

One he would never forget.

CHAPTER TEN

Rebecca

She woke before dawn, all at once, waking from a dream where she was standing in a burning house, trying to put out a fire with the sprayer at the sink. The smoke and flames were closing in.

Her heart was pounding fast as she wrenched out of the dream. She stared at the unfamiliar ceiling as she remembered everything that had led to her lying here in the arms of two sexy men. Two kind, funny, and hot-as-hell men who also happened to be wildly successful. And they were naked. And they were naked with her in a bed.

She remembered every second, every kiss, every touch. She remembered very clearly how it had felt to be taken by them both at the same time. How the pleasure had nearly broken her mind and left her a puddle of sated bliss.

Oh God, she was such a slut. The first date, she'd thrown herself at them. And Jack Meacham. She had actually believed he didn't mean to put her shop out of business. Was she insane? Had it been the wine?

No, she couldn't blame the wine. This was all on her.

She froze, her mind racing. She needed to leave. Now. Something like panic twisted around her. Her heart was pounding even faster, and it was hard to breathe. Carefully, she managed to squirm out from under Jack's arm without waking him. She managed to shift away from Liam too. Moving slowly, she eased her way off the bed, climbing off from the foot of the bed so she wouldn't wake either of them.

Jack stirred anyway, giving an adorable little snore and rolling closer to Liam. The two naked men lay there together, still sleeping soundly, still looking perfect together. They wouldn't miss her...because she didn't belong with them.

She quickly snatched up her clothes from everywhere they'd been tossed. She panicked when she couldn't find her panties anywhere, but she finally found them hanging on a small dracaena tree-shrub thing. That's right. They'd gone flying when she slid them down and kicked them off.

Once she was dressed, she moved toward the bedroom door. Then she stopped.

Was she doing the right thing?

No. But she wasn't sure there was a right thing now. Last night...last night had been magical. Unforgettable. But mornings were for regrets. For second thoughts. If she saw either Jack or Liam looking at her over coffee with regrets or second thoughts in their eyes, it would crush her heart into dust.

She needed to go. She would make it easy for them. They loved each other, and she was just a distraction for them. A flash in the pan. Something to spice up their love life for a little while.

Rebecca took one last long look at them

because... Hell, why try to put a noble face on it? Because they were naked. Because they looked so hot and sexy, all those muscles and bare skin and of course those two cocks that had driven her wild last night. Liam's butt was so squeezable and firm that her hand lifted as if she meant to do just that. But she snatched her hand back. It would only wake him up. And she couldn't face them right now.

She just couldn't.

Rebecca turned and hurried through the bedroom door. She got turned around in the mansion and ended up in the kitchen. Her stomach grumbled, so she took one banana from a fruit bowl and returned to her quest for the front door.

Her pocketbook was on the table in the foyer. She remembered putting it there so she wouldn't forget it—and it was amazing that she'd had the sense to think that clearly. They'd been kissing her at the time. The way they'd been touching her had been driving her wild.

She let herself out...and realized she didn't have a car. And they'd sent the limo away last night.

Crap.

Looks like it was a taxi or a ride service for her. She couldn't exactly flee on foot. Well, she could, but it would be absurd.

She still felt guilty. Guilty for stealing out on them. As if she was ashamed of what they'd done.

When she'd woken up, she'd called herself a slut. But that wasn't because she'd slept with two men at once, no matter how decadent and greedy that might sound. It was because she'd fallen into bed with them on the first date. She never did that. She didn't have hang-ups about sex. She'd lost her virginity in high school. She was open-minded—and she'd proved it by sleeping with two bisexual men. But she also believed (in theory anyway) in not jumping into things too quickly. And physical intimacy was one of those things.

But at the time, it had felt right. It had felt like the perfect ending to a perfect night.

What would they think of her now? Giving it up on the first date, even though she'd warned them she wouldn't. Where was her womanly pride?

Well, they'd proven her wrong after all, and she didn't want to deal with the fallout from her choice. Because right now she could leave and still keep the good memories of a really wild night. But if she stayed...if they looked at her differently...it would destroy those memories forever. She would only be able to focus on feeling like a girl who'd given away the farm on the very first date, judging herself, second-guessing everything...

God, would you shut up about that already, she scolded herself. *It's not the 1800s. Don't be such a prude. Now go back into the kitchen, make yourself some coffee, wait for them to wake up, and don't feel a bit of shame.*

Yes. Good points. *Great* points, in fact. She should listen to herself.

Instead, she walked out the front door. She hurried down the driveway, nearly running. Then she was on the street. These were all fancy houses. She might be a little disheveled from waking up and fleeing without showering, wrinkled dress and all, but she still looked as if she belonged in this neighborhood. Sort of. If people didn't look too closely.

She expected a shout from behind her at any moment. She expected Liam or Jack standing on the balcony, calling out to her. And they would be naked and not caring because they were so desperate to call her back.

But no one called her name.

It was stupid to feel broken up about that, but her throat tightened anyway, and she was already blinking back tears.

Stupid. Stupid. *Stupid*. That's what she was. A stupid, emotional woman. She should never have fallen for their charms.

She hurried down the sidewalk, wanting to get a block away before calling for a ride service to take her back to Fremont. That trip would cost an arm and a leg, but what other choice did she have? She could call one of her girlfriends, but they would want to talk. They'd want the juicy details. They would look at her as if she were crazy—or stupid—for running out on something like this.

And they would probably be right.

The worst part of it was simple. She'd had such a wonderful, unforgettable time. Too wonderful. That scared her. Maybe she was right to stop things from going any farther, because they would never work out. The odds...and the world...were against them. She didn't want to be hurt. And she didn't want them to have to hurt her.

So she was right to end it before she lost any more of her heart to them. The chemistry between them had been too intense. Something that good would never last. Even with Jack, a man who had rubbed her the wrong way since the moment she'd met him, things had turned out so wildly different. So wonderful good. And last night, he had rubbed her all the right ways.

It was best to leave on that note. They could think about her fondly. She might be another notch on their bedposts, but they were a notch on hers too. Liam was one of those sweetheart men who were also sexually ravenous in bed, and that was great. But she knew that with Jack, with the fact that he was starting Lighthouse Bakery, that unresolved tension would eventually ruin things. It had to.

See? She was already worried about her business again...

No, she couldn't think about that right now. If she did, she would probably have some kind of mental breakdown.

With shaking hands, she used an app to order a ride back to Fremont. She sat down on a low stone wall that encircled one of the big, fancy houses with its immaculate yard. She hoped the homeowner didn't call the cops on her, although the sun was just beginning to brighten the horizon, and she hadn't seen a car on the quiet streets yet.

The fifteen-minute wait time felt like six hours. She kept expecting to see Jack's Benz driving down the street as if they were desperately chasing her down. She burst out with a laugh that sounded more like a cry of pain. She shook her head. She didn't have any right to self-pity. She had made her bed, and she would sleep in it.

The Saturday morning streets in his exclusive neighborhood remained empty until the ride-sharing taxi arrived. The drive back to Fremont seemed three times as long as when she'd come to Portland riding in the back of a limo. The driver tried to make some idle conversation with her. She was polite but not very forthcoming. She kept thinking the driver somehow knew this was a walk of shame—or ride of shame— back home from a ritzy neighborhood to her straight-up blue-collar neighborhood.

It shouldn't bother her. Why should she care

what some stranger thought? She didn't.

No, this was mostly about her. Her messed up mental state.

She wasn't going to go to open the shop today. She couldn't. What if Liam and Jack showed up and wanted to talk? All the clichés said that women loved to talk, especially about relationships, but right now that just felt like pouring salt into an open wound.

Finally, they turned onto her street. The driver let her off in front of her apartment. She went inside. Everything seemed so quiet.

It was forty minutes later when her cell phone began to ring. Her heart began to slam in her chest at the sound. Either that was the most obnoxious early morning spam call ever, or that was Jack or Liam, calling to find out where she had gone.

Her hands were shaking badly as she lifted the phone and checked the number. It was Liam.

She almost didn't answer. She closed her eyes, her throat tightening up, feeling absolutely wretched. Her thumb hovered over the red phone icon to reject the call.

Don't be a coward. Answer his call.

She swiped to answer. "Hello, Liam."

"Rebecca, thank God. I was worried."

Guilt stabbed through her. Leaving had been a mistake. A selfish mistake. She'd only been thinking about herself. Those simple words from Liam made it clear to her in a very stark way.

"I'm sorry. It was wrong to walk out like that, but..." She trailed off because she didn't have the first idea where to begin.

There was a long silence from Liam. "It's a bit overwhelming, right?" He sounded so understanding that she immediately teared up. "It's my fault. We jumped into it too fast. But I can't say I'm sorry for what happened last night. I won't cheapen it. It was amazing."

She took a deep, shuddering breath. She agreed in every way possible. Only she couldn't get herself to say it to him. Because that would give him an opening. To see her. To talk. And right now she only wanted to...to what? To cry under the covers? To be left alone to lick her wounds? To somehow convince herself that she'd done the right thing?

"I think it's best if we just leave it as an

incredible memory. Best for all three of us."

"Where are you?" he said, and she could hear the edge of panic in his voice. Panic she had caused. "Let me come see you."

"No, Liam. I don't think that's a good idea. I really don't."

"I don't want to talk about this over the phone. And look, you're too important to me and Jack to just walk away from now."

She gave a bitter laugh. "We had one date. And a great fuck. It's not like we're married now. Look, this is on me. You don't have to feel guilty." Her eyes burned with tears, but she managed to keep her voice from revealing her pain. "Besides, I thought guys preferred to screw and run?"

"That's not me. And that's not Jack. I deserve a chance to prove that to you."

He was right. He deserved that chance. But she couldn't give it to him. Because even though she'd been the one to say that stuff about one date and all of that, she knew she could happily lose her heart to these two men. Falling in love with them would be easy. Too easy.

No, all she could do was repeat herself. "That's not a good idea. Goodbye, Liam. Please, don't make this harder for any of us. Don't...don't come looking for me, okay?"

"I can't make that promise."

"You should." She disconnected and put the phone down with hands shaking so badly she nearly dropped it.

She took a shower. She didn't know what else to do. Her head was spinning with all her conflicting thoughts, and her heart hurt as if someone were squeezing it. She turned the water on hot, standing under the stream, trying not to think of anything right now.

She stood there until the hot water ran out. When she was standing under the stream of water, there was no way to see her tears.

CHAPTER ELEVEN

Liam

What the hell had gone wrong?

He slowly lowered his phone and set it on the counter as if it were something that might explode. Right now, he felt like it *had* exploded.

They hadn't argued. They hadn't fought. She hadn't even raised her voice. But after that call, he felt like he'd gone ten rounds with a heavyweight boxer.

Jack's face was just as grim. He was leaning up against the opposite counter in their big kitchen with his arms crossed. Morning light streamed in through the windows. The light made his bare chest and skin appear golden. It highlighted his hair and made the color in his eyes really pop. Another time, Liam would've been irresistibly drawn over to kiss him because he looked so damn good.

But right now he was still reeling.

Jack was watching him, his eyes both angry and sympathetic.

"She doesn't want to talk," he said, and it wasn't a question.

"She asked me not to go see her. She wants to end it."

"Because of me."

"She blamed herself. Not you."

Jack shook his head. "I think we both know this is about me. I got off on the wrong foot with her. I was a jerk. She's afraid Lighthouse might put her out of business. I can't blame her for having second thoughts. She has every right to hate my guts."

"Does she have to worry about Lighthouse?" Liam demanded.

"I told you, she doesn't. She's a niche cookie shop. Lighthouse will make cookies, sure, but we make pastries and bread and all kinds of baked goods. Besides, her product is really good. I could make her millions if she let me help her push her cookies on the world." He shook his head, his expression bitter. "But right now, I don't think there's anything I can do to reassure her." He ran a hand through his hair. "I tried last night to reassure her in every way I could. It didn't work."

"I can't think of anything we did wrong. The three of us together? It was fucking amazing."

"Maybe I'm just an arrogant bastard," Jack said. "But I don't think she had any complaints. But it looks like the second-guessing starts the morning after."

Liam always took an easy outlook on life. He didn't get bothered by traffic jams or junk mail or people talking at the movies. He didn't sweat the small stuff, and about the big stuff, he really believed things would turn out all right. People were generally good, even though they sometimes had to be reminded of that goodness. He had faith in humanity, in life. He was usually very Zen. Jack even teased him about it to no end.

But right now, he felt lost. He felt restless, almost panicked. The feeling hit him even harder because he wasn't used to it. After all, nothing much bothered him.

But losing Rebecca did.

He slammed his fist down on the counter and cursed.

Jack's eyes went wide. "Whoa, whoa, kid. What the hell is going on? The only time I've ever seen you this upset was when we got into a bar fight with that homophobe in Cincinnati."

He let out a long breath, managing to get control of himself. His stomach still felt cold and twisted up in knots. "You're right. Yeah, you're right. I just thought..." He shook his head, beginning to pace. "I thought we had her. What the hell is wrong with me? I told her on the phone that we moved too fast. Looks like I was right."

"We didn't pressure her, Liam."

"We didn't slow things down either."

"No, we didn't," Jack said, looking at him fiercely. "You know why? Because it felt right."

"Yeah." He paced to the sink, poured himself some water, and then didn't drink it. He wasn't thirsty. He just wanted something to do with his hands.

"She made her choice, Liam. We need to respect it."

He glanced at Jack. "Why are you so calm about this? You're the one who gets all riled up. You never let anything stop you. Was she just a fun roll in the hay for you?"

Jack's expression darkened. "Not at all. How the hell could you think that of me?"

"Because I don't understand how you can be so calm about this. I mean, I have this feeling we're supposed to be together. Like we fit."

"I'm not surprised you believe in that love at-first-sight stuff."

"And you don't? What about us? It was the same thing for me. When we met again. After college..."

"I'm not going to say I didn't want you from the moment I first saw you, because that would be a total lie. But we *built* what we have. It didn't just spring into being."

He paced back to the other side of the kitchen, knowing Jack was right. "I want to see her again. It's eating away at me."

"Listen. Give her some space. If she still doesn't want anything to do with us after a few days, it's her choice. We need to respect what she wants."

"What she wants is wrong. She doesn't know you like I know you." He shook his head. When he'd fallen asleep with Rebecca in his arms and Jack right there, he'd been so happy. Everything had felt so perfect. To have it all yanked away so suddenly only made him want it more.

"That might not matter," Jack said. "Not everyone's cool with this kind of arrangement. You know that."

His eyes narrowed. "What do you mean?"

"You know what I mean. Us. A woman. Three people together, two of them men who also love each other. Don't play dumb."

"I'm not playing dumb. I just refuse to give up on her so easily. I refuse to believe this is some kind of sudden prejudice about how we choose to rock and roll in the bedroom."

"And I hate seeing you so broken up about this. We made our interest known. Hell, we couldn't have been clearer. Now it's up to her. She's the one who left this morning, not us."

Listening to Jack was only frustrating him, making him angry. "I'm going to go see her."

Jack frowned. "She told you not to. Give her some space."

"This is important." He started toward the door leading from the kitchen.

Jack caught his arm, halting him. "Liam. *Don't*. Trust me on this."

He wrenched away. "What the hell is wrong with you, Jack? You chased after this dream of building a factory in Maine harder than this. I can't believe you're going to let her walk out of our lives and do nothing."

"It's her choice. We're all adults. She made her choice. Respect it."

Liam didn't say anything. He walked out of the kitchen.

"You're making a mistake," Jack called after him. "But I'll be here when she turns you down."

Liam still didn't reply. He couldn't. He was too upset.

He walked into the four-car garage, glanced at the Benz, and took the Ferrari instead. A few seconds later, he was out of the driveway and speeding down the road.

But after five minutes, he took a turn and, instead of heading to Fremont, he headed for the harbor where his sailboat, *Easy Rider*, was berthed. Why? Because the more he calmed down and thought about it, the more he believed Jack had a point—at least about giving her some space. He didn't like how the conversation between them had gone down, but Jack was clearly seeing things better than he was right now.

He needed to clear his head. To find his center again. What better place than on the water? The sun. The waves. There wasn't a hint of last night's fog anywhere. The morning was beautiful and bright, with a hint of New England autumn in the air.

An hour later, he was at the helm, sails up and full of wind. The wind off the water smelled of salt. As he guided his sailing yacht across the water, he felt his tension, stress, and worry slowly easing away.

He could think out here. Away from the rush of the city, the noise, the hubbub, he could quickly find his calm center and balance himself.

Now he needed to decide what he wanted.

He was rich. He had a man he loved. He had a yacht to escape it all when he needed to.

He was damn lucky, and he knew it.

But he wanted Rebecca too. He had felt the connection with her. The power and chemistry between the three of them. It seemed to be ordained by the universe, the way everything had fallen into place. Yeah, that sounded cheesy as hell, but no one was here to laugh at him for thinking it either.

Not only was Rebecca exactly the kind of funny, kind, warm, girl-next-door beauty he'd always been attracted to, but she was adventurous enough to throw herself into a threesome with two men who already had a relationship. He admired that. It took bravery, some deep down self-confidence.

But...was that why she had run away this morning? Was she not as adventurous as he'd thought? Had she just been caught up in the moment? The sexual tension had been intense from the moment they'd escorted her to the limo. That had been his fault. And Jack's, though Jack would never apologize for it. And come to think of it, Liam wouldn't apologize for it either. He was attracted to her in a very natural, very real way. There was nothing wrong with that. Nothing to regret.

His only regret was not being awake this morning to be there for her when she obviously needed someone to talk to.

So could this be salvaged? Was he the only one who believed in it?

Right now, he was the most frustrated with Jack, not Rebecca. The man built companies and corporations, and now he was all about "giving her space?" He hadn't given her space when he'd kissed her. Liam wasn't jealous of that—not even a little—but Jack's behavior in the kitchen this morning had bothered him deeply. Jack was always the more passionate guy, always getting riled up, driven, that classic type-A personality. So where had that fight, that drive gone?

Because this morning, their roles had been reversed. It disturbed him. Especially with Jack suddenly playing the role of "the calm voice of reason" when so much was on the line. He knew Jack was upset about her leaving too. He could read the man at a glance. But he was still hiding his feelings beneath this sudden mask of indifference. Why?

Could it be that he really, deeply cared for her too? As much as Liam, maybe more? And was that show in the kitchen after the call his way of hiding that? Of hiding the pain he was feeling?

Maybe. It meant that Liam had to find his patience again and be more understanding. He wasn't alone in this, after all.

The wind was shifting. He worked the sails, turning to recapture the wind, getting the sails full again, keeping up his speed. The *Easy Rider* cut across the water like a knife. She was moving fast and free, and out here on the wide expanse of ocean, with huge white clouds on the horizon, there was nothing better.

He wanted to share this with Rebecca. He was certain she would love sailing. He didn't know why, he just had a feeling.

Like the feeling that she was perfect for them.

That was it. He was not going to give up on her. She might push him away, but he would be patient. He would prove to her that his feelings were real and deep, not just a flash in the pan for a one-night stand. He would convince her to give them another chance. To let go of any fears or feelings of shame and simply live life day by day. Taking joy in the little things.

Because love, in all its forms, was the finest thing on Earth. You didn't need to be a scientist or a philosopher to understand that. You understood it in your heart.

Tomorrow he would go see Rebecca. He would invite her sailing. If she said no or refused to see him, he would leave quietly.

And the next day he would do the same. Until he convinced her to take a chance. Until he proved himself to her.

What about Jack, though? Was he still game? Or had he given up on her?

Liam knew he needed to be careful. Somehow, he needed to prove to both Jake and Rebecca that the three of them had a chance together. Being mad or frustrated with either of them was pointless and helped nothing. He'd always known that, but he'd had to come out here to remind himself again.

Smiling, he felt filled with renewed purpose. He felt like he could be the link between Rebecca and Jack, binding the three of them tightly together. Both of them were powerful personalities. Headstrong. You could even say stubborn. Always acting before thinking of the consequences. Throwing themselves all-in with something. Leaping before they looked.

The memory of Jack running his hands along Rebecca's beautiful body still stirred him even now. The image of him kissing her warmed his heart. He wanted more of that. He wanted it for the rest of their lives.

The *Easy Rider* dipped into a trough and then shot upward again, the bow cresting through a big wave. Ocean spray misted around him. He laughed with delight.

Maybe he was crazy to try this. He wasn't a wet-behind-the-ears kid anymore, and he recognized the real thing, even after a very short time. It wasn't anything logical. It wasn't a list of attributes to tick off.

It was something deeper than all of that. Mysterious and yet powerful.

He was going to go with his heart. He was going to bring Rebecca back to them, and he was going to make this thing between them work.

No matter what.

CHAPTER TWELVE

Jack

It was late afternoon, almost evening, when he drove to the docks to find Liam. Jack had been on edge all day, ever since waking up this morning to find Rebecca gone from their bed. Not to mention the tense argument with Liam.

Liam had been upset—more upset than Jack had seen him in a very long time. That made Jack angry, even though he'd done his best to hide it this morning. It made him angry with Rebecca for hurting him. For hurting them both.

The truth was, he'd been shocked to find her gone. He'd hoped to spend the day with her and Liam. Hell, it might sound sappy, but he'd been eager to learn everything about her and to let her get to know him and Liam. They'd had so much physical chemistry in the bedroom, an intimacy that rocked him with its power, and he wanted that same level of intimacy in knowing all about her too.

Instead, she'd ditched them. He'd never had that happen before—women or men—and he'd certainly never done it to anyone else.

It was a blow to the ego. It humiliated and hurt him. Worst of all, it had upset Liam. So while Liam had been planning how to make this right, it had been all Jack could do to hide his fury over the situation.

He'd been right after all. Rebecca Johnson had been nothing but trouble from the get-go.

Even though that was true, he still wanted her. He didn't know if that meant he was crazy or just plain stupid. Probably both.

So Rebecca had vanished without a word, hurt them both, and caused a damn-near fight between him and Liam. But all of that could be forgiven and forgotten. He wasn't vindictive, but what really and truly bothered him was that she had hurt Liam enough to have him acting so out of character. Jack was tough enough to have his heart broken over and over again by any woman on the planet, but when someone hurt the man he loved...

Or maybe he was overstating things. Boasting. Talking shit. Because now that he thought about it, losing Liam would crush him beyond all repair. Given the intensity of the passion between the three of them, Rebecca might easily mean the same to him very soon. Things had already been a whirlwind, but sometimes with these whirlwind passions, people got busted up. They made a mistake, they had regrets. People got hurt.

He turned down the street leading to the waterfront. The harbor was in view. The water was choppy and dark. The beautiful morning had given over to uglier weather. He parked in one of the lots and walked toward the pier, shoving his hands in his pockets. The air held a crispness to it. Autumn was coming fast. A few of the red maples he saw were starting to lose their leaves even this early.

Soon the days would be short and cold. It was ironic. When he was off somewhere hot or humid with Liam, say rainforests or Northern Africa, he always missed Maine winters. But when he was actually enduring a New England winter, he started thinking longingly about Florida or the Caribbean or the southern coast of France.

Did that mean he couldn't be happy? Ever? Was he doomed to simply chase things for the rest of his life? Like this big bakery he was building. Once he had that finished, what came next? Why couldn't he be as relaxed and even-keeled as Liam?

Although right now, neither of them were relaxed. He snorted. It was all because of some woman. What a cliché.

No, you jerk, he corrected himself. *Not* some *woman. Rebecca.*

That was right. It was almost frightening how drawn to her they were. Being with Rebecca had been like getting behind the wheel of a car that could go zero to sixty in three seconds and then stomping on the gas.

But now he was worried they'd raced up to high speeds and drove the car off a cliff. Not only was he upset about missing a chance to have Rebecca in their lives, but he worried this might come between him and Liam. That possibility only made things even more fraught and difficult.

He wanted to slow down. He wanted to have some time to sort this out. He wanted to give Rebecca time to settle down, time to miss them and second-guess her choices. Liam was right. They had moved too fast. It was clear to him now. But at the time, everything had felt right. The chemistry, the passion had been undeniable. It was the fallout that was causing problems now.

Jack believed they should let it settle and then start again on romancing her. Taking their time. Letting her adjust. Letting her again fit into their existing relationship, making it stronger, bringing new life, a different perspective, a whole new energy.

Or if she truly didn't want anything to do with them, then he would let her go. Her choice. But he would be there for Liam to pick up the pieces afterward.

Yeah. All of that was easier said than done. Because he didn't think his Laidback Liam was having any of it. That was unsettling, because Jack was usually the one racing ahead, while Liam remained calm, relaxed, and took the long view of things. Rebecca had upended everything in their lives. He had never played this role before, having to temper Liam's desires with a cold splash of reality.

His smartphone ringtone suddenly went off, startling him. He pulled the phone from his pocket quickly, thinking it might be Liam or maybe even Rebecca.

But no, it was Susie Ford, his head of marketing and sales. He considered letting the call go to voicemail, but he couldn't. Even though he was in no mood to deal with work stuff, he had a responsibility to the people he employed. Decisions needed to be made. He needed to make them.

"What can I do for you, Susie?"

"Jack. Glad to reach you. I have some great news."

That perked him up a little. "Go ahead. I could use some."

"We just secured supply accounts with a top restaurant in Portland, a coffee shop in Westbrook, and the two biggest restaurants in Fremont. I also made an offer to a few other places, and I think they can be brought around with some savvy negotiating. Our competitive prices are winning us accounts left, right, and sideways."

"Good, good," he said, knowing he had to say something positive because she had worked hard on this. But at the moment, winning a few accounts supplying bread or desserts to a handful of restaurants didn't seem like that big a deal. In fact, it felt like more of a distraction or an annoyance when he was dealing with his love life spiraling down the toilet. True, it was good that they'd already have waiting customers for when they opened their doors, but it was hard to get that excited about it right now. "Tell the sales team excellent work. Was that everything?"

"That's it for now," Susie said brightly, although he could tell she was a little confused. She'd probably expected a stronger reaction. She deserved a better one, she really did. It was just that he was all torn up about this thing with Rebecca leaving and with Liam this morning that he couldn't really focus on work right now. "I know you're busy. I'll let you go."

"Thanks, Susie. Keep me updated. Tell the team to expect some bonuses for their hard work."

That brightened her up some. "I will. I'm sure they'll be happy to hear it."

He signed off and put away the smartphone. Already the conversation was fading from his mind, replaced by the other problems he had on his hands right now.

The *Easy Rider* was in tied up in its berth. Earlier, he had called Liam to make sure he'd be back from his sailing jaunt. The weather had brought him back to port sooner than Liam had probably liked. It was no surprise after all that had happened in the past few days that Liam had come here to take his sailboat out on the waves.

Jack crossed the dock, leaning on one of the pier piling tops. He spotted Liam on deck near the far side of the stern cleaning the wood rails to remove the salt spray. "Hey, sailor. Permission to come aboard?"

Liam left the railing walked over to him, his expression serious. His skin was so tanned it almost looked fake. But damn was the man gorgeous.

"Permission granted," Liam said.

Jack moved toward the gangplank and crossed over the dark, choppy water. Liam hadn't been smiling, which was rare, but his voice hadn't sounded upset. He looked calm again.

Now here Jack was to destroy that calm. Because they had to come to some kind of agreement about Rebecca. Whether to keep perusing her...or to give her what she wanted and let her go.

He walked over to Liam and kissed him gently. Liam allowed it, but he didn't linger in Jack's embrace. That wasn't a good sign.

"Want a beer?" Liam asked, walking toward the stairs leading below deck. "I've got plenty of cold ones."

"A beer would be heaven right now."

Liam went below, grabbed two bottles, and came back onto the deck. He handed a bottle to Jack.

"To having no regrets," Liam said, raising his bottle.

"I'll drink to that." They *clinked* the bottles together. Jack took a long swig of his. It was cold and tasted good going down. He let out a long sigh.

"I'm sorry about this morning," Liam said. "I

was out of control."

Jack shook his head. "If that was you out of control, you're still far better than I am. You barely raised your voice. I don't remember a lot of swearing and waving your arms around." He lifted his beer bottle again with a smirk. "So no apologies are necessary. You're still a better man than me."

"Listen to you. You're so full of crap you squeak. You're a good man. You care about people, about the community. You're doing everything you can to bring back industry to this part of the state. So you care. It's one of the many reasons I love you."

"All right, all right. I'll accept your compliment. But I'm sorry things were tense this morning. I know I didn't do or say the right things to defuse it. Usually, I rely on you to do that." He rubbed the back of his neck. "Turns out, I'm not very good at it. I hate admitting that too."

They were quiet for a few moments. It was a comfortable kind of quiet. It was easy to relax around Liam. The man could stir his blood with a touch, a look, or a few naughty words. But most of the time, being with Liam was a comfort, like being on an extended vacation, lying on a beach somewhere with a cold beer in one hand and not a care—or cell phone—in the world.

He glanced at Liam. "Will you take me out on the water tomorrow? I feel like I need to get away for a while."

"I understand. I'd love to take you sailing. After I go to see Rebecca. I'll take you both out."

Jack hesitated. Now that he was faced with Liam's certainty, he was having doubts of his own again. "She might not agree, Liam. She wants something else. I don't know. I'm sure it's me who is driving her away. But I'm too greedy to give you up, Liam. Ever."

"You don't have to. Ever."

"Good. And I have feelings for Rebecca. I really do. I'm not going to be coy about it—she's someone I could come to love. As much as I love you. Everything's there...even the chemistry. But she has to feel the same. If she left us, then maybe she doesn't."

"I told you this morning, I'm not willing to give up on her. The three of us have a chance at something amazing and powerful and unique. I won't let it go without a fight."

"I think you're right. But I also don't know how to make that happen." He hated to admit to any failing, any weakness. But it was true. He was dragging his heels on this, making excuses, because he was afraid.

"Maybe you should tell her how you feel for starters."

"Didn't I show her last night? Shouldn't my actions speak for themselves? We were honest and upfront with her about everything." He paused. "Or maybe we really did move too fast. She didn't give us a chance to write her poetry or anything."

Liam snorted and shook his head. "You're not helping, talking like that. I know you're still angry."

"Angry? Yeah...you're right." He leaned against the railing, looking out over the choppy water. "But I've been thinking about this morning. You were right, and I was wrong. I was angry at Rebecca and trying to hide it."

"I'm not angry at her," Liam said. "My heart goes out to her. I don't want her to feel like she made some kind of mistake. Or blame herself. Or...hell, I don't know. I want her to have no regrets." Liam ran a hand through his wind-blown hair, dismay on his face. "I wanted to make her happy, and it's clear that we didn't."

Damn it. "That's why I was upset with her. Because you're kicking your own ass over losing her. As if we drove her away. Hell, maybe we did move too fast, but she made her choices too."

Liam looked at him sharply. "And that's just it. I don't want her to have those regrets. I wanted to prove that we would be good for her, but then I couldn't be a man and hold my desires in check. I was thinking with my little head, and it fucked up everything."

"So was I," Jack said. "I wanted her, and you, just as badly. And cut us some slack, Liam. We wouldn't be the first men to think with our cocks and have it screw everything up."

But he could see Liam wasn't buying it. He was already shaking his head. "But we're better than that. And that's what we needed to prove to her. And that's where we failed."

"What do they say on motivational posters? Failure is just another mile marker on the road to success? I could probably think of a bunch of inspirational quotes." He moved closer, put one arm around Liam's shoulders, and kissed him tenderly. "I love you. You have the biggest heart of anyone I've ever met. Except maybe Rebecca. You could be neck and neck with her; the jury's still out. I don't deserve you. But I'm determined to keep you."

Liam broke into a smile that slowly spread across his handsome face. "I guess I'll keep you too. You and your cheesy inspirational quotes."

"I should write a book filled with sappy inspirational quotes and make the world a better place. But before I do, we need to plan how we're going to get Rebecca back."

Liam met his gaze, hope and love in his eyes. "You still want her? You said you were angry with her..."

"I was. Because she hurt you. Only a very special woman could make my relaxed, come-what-may lover lose his cool like you did this morning. But I'm only human. Seeing you upset, seeing you hurt, makes me angry. Hell, she hurt me too, just as I was starting to fall for her. But she's special. We both feel it. I was just a little slower to realize it. And maybe—just maybe—I almost screwed it up from the get-go by being an ass. So if I can come around, so can she."

Liam dragged him into a fierce kiss. He embraced Jack tightly. Jack simply let himself go, losing himself in the embrace, in the kiss, loving every second of it.

After the kiss, Liam stayed close, looking into Jack's eyes. "Thank you."

"Don't thank me. I didn't do anything."

"Thank you anyway."

He took a deep breath. "What are you going to do if she says no again?" he asked carefully, hating to break the mood. But it had to be said. "What if she flat out refuses to see us? It's a possibility."

"We need to make sure she doesn't say no."

"That's not an answer. Not really."

Liam looked him dead in the eyes. "Fine. If she really wants nothing to do with us even after we pour our hearts out and make the case why it should be the three of us against the world...then I'll have no choice but to accept it and move on. There. Is that what you wanted to hear?"

"I didn't want to hear it. But I needed to hear it."

He gently touched Liam's face. "You'll still have me, Liam. Always."

Liam closed his eyes, leaning into his touch. "I know. I'm a lucky man. I shouldn't be greedy."

A surprised laugh burst from Jack's lips. "You? Greedy? You're one of the most generous people I know."

"Maybe. But right now I don't think anyone could say I'm not at least a little greedy. I have a man who loves me—a guy I love to death—and here I am chasing after a woman who left us high and dry."

"I'm the one who should have given her a chance to explain, Liam. We're adults. We should be able to talk to each other like adults. I shouldn't have been so quick to turn my back on her after she left. I wasn't thinking clearly this morning."

Liam glanced at him, frowning. "What do you mean?"

"I mean, it's true I was upset that you were upset. But part of me was hurt and angry at her rejection. I guess I got put in my place. I'm not used to people turning me down."

Liam nodded, looking thoughtful. "It does prove

she's no gold-digger, though. Were you worried about that?"

He shrugged. "I wasn't really. We both know the type, and Rebecca's definitely not that type. That's part of what drew us to her in the first place, right?"

"Right."

"So I wasn't thinking clearly this morning, but now I am. She belongs with us, and between the two of us, we can bring her back where she belongs."

"Good. Because I feel exactly the same," Liam replied, giving him that charming smile that Jack simply adored. "It's too late to go to her tonight. But tomorrow…"

"Tomorrow it is. We'll go to her shop. She can't throw us out if we're well-behaved, paying customers."

"I think legally she probably can, Jack."

He waved away those concerns. "She'll give us a chance, though. So let's have another beer and watch the sunset together. Then I'm going to drag you below deck for some fun." His grin was almost predatory. "For old time's sake. Because after we win her heart back tomorrow, it will be the three of us from then until eternity."

"We might need a bigger bed."

"Luckily, we're filthy rich. I'll have a custom one built. Anything else?"

"Will you still love me after I get fat from eating all her cookies?"

Jack punched him on the arm. "Of course I will, you idiot." He pulled Liam into another fierce kiss. When the kiss was over, it had left them both breathless. Breathless, but all the tension between them was gone. "Now come on. Let's sit down and enjoy another beer together. Then I'm going to show you exactly how much I love you. That's a promise."

CHAPTER THIRTEEN

Rebecca

It was morning. She was in her Cookie Nookie mobile, making the morning deliveries. She had the music turned up loud, rattling the speakers. Loud music was helping her *not* to think about anything. Certainly not about Liam and Jack or how much she missed them. How much she wanted to call them, to see them, to kiss them again…

No. She wasn't going to think about that. It was too soon. It all hurt too much.

She parked and opened the back. She got out the daily delivery for Deer Park Bistro four boxes of chocolate chip supreme cookies. She carried them to the side door, which was left open for the restaurant's morning setup and prep crew.

After dropping off the cookies in one of the walk-in fridges, she paused to say hello to Jim, the day shift manager. He was washing vegetables in one of the big sinks in back.

"Hi, Jim. Just letting you know the cookies are in the usual place."

Jim looked up from the sink, grabbed a white kitchen towel, and quickly dried off his hands. He actually looked upset…and a little guilty. That was weird.

"Hey, Rebecca. Um. Do you have a minute? I need to tell you something."

Her heart went to ice so fast she might as well have fallen into a frozen lake. His tone, everything about this was wrong.

"Sure, what is it?"

"Look, there's no easy way to say this, but I wanted to give you the head's up as soon as I could.

The owner...well, starting next month, he's going to be buying chocolate chip cookies from Lighthouse Bakery. After they open." Jim frowned. "I told him the cookies weren't going to be as good, but he thinks they're 'good enough for us.' Hell, he's being a cheapskate, trying to save a few bucks."

"I see." She felt like she had a fishbone stuck in her throat. She finally managed to swallow, and the motion hurt her throat, even though it was empty. "Thank you...for letting me know. Do you think it would do any good to talk to him?"

Jim rubbed his chin, looking more distressed than ever. "You could try, but I'm not sure you could match Lighthouse's prices. They're pretty cheap. I don't want to see you get screwed trying to keep us as a client."

"Ah." She really didn't know what to say. She'd been working with Deer Park Bistro for years now. She had to fight back a sudden attack of tears. She was not going to start bawling and embarrass herself right now. She *refused*. "I... Okay, just...let me know the last day you need cookies delivered. Tell Leo I understand and thanks for being such a longtime customer. Cookie

Nookie will still be around if he decides he wants to switch back."

That might be a wild untruth. If Lighthouse stole all her customers, she could easily find herself bankrupt and on the unemployment line in three months.

Rebecca made it all the way out to her car with her head held high and her eyes dry. Inside the car was a different story. Her vision blurred, and she let out one painful sob. Her hands were shaking, so she tightened them ruthlessly on the steering wheel.

She allowed herself thirty seconds of feeling absolutely miserable before getting herself under control again.

She checked her makeup, touched herself up with still-trembling hands, and started the car.

If her heart had been broken after leaving Liam and Jack, now it was crushed to a fine powder. This was all on Jack. The man was obviously full of crap, telling her that Lighthouse wasn't going to put her out of business. Then he went behind her back and stole one of her best clients. She needed that account, dammit! He had undercut her because he could. He didn't care if he drove a small business under. It was all about profit and success for that man.

She should've known better. She never should've believed him when he'd showed up and lured her on that date. He'd bamboozled her with that unexpected kiss. She should have slapped him.

She should have beaten him with a broom and chased him out into traffic. She should have —

Oh God, I can't believe I actually slept with him. I slept with the enemy, and I wasn't even drunk!

It was going to be years before she lived this one down. Every word Jack Meacham had said had been a lie to get her to sleep with them.

Her one single point of pride was the fact that she'd left them before they could ditch her.

She started the car, exited the parking lot, and headed to her next delivery. Her lungs felt full of ice-crystals and dread. Was she going to find the same thing when she got to the Royale Restaurant and Bar? This was the last client on her daily list. Another account she relied on to make ends meet and stay in the black.

After parking, she picked up the cookie delivery

and headed inside on unsteady legs. As weak as her legs felt, she also felt strangely numb. Her head felt numb. All the hurt and sadness and anger from just a few minutes ago seemed to have frozen her into a numbness that she couldn't shake.

She put away the cookies in Royale's walk-in cooler and went immediately to the dayshift manager. Her name was Tina. She was from Texas. That was how she remembered Tina's name. Tina from Texas. Ha. Ha.

God, she was losing her shit. It would be scary if she didn't feel so numb right now.

"Hi, Tina," she said, leaning against the office door. "Just made the daily delivery. Say, am I still going to have your business next month or not?"

Well, that was certainly more direct than she'd intended. Her mouth had opened and those awkward, brash words had poured out. Maybe she should just go home. Hide under the covers. No, under the bed. Today was turning out to be a disaster.

Tina blinked at her and frowned a little. "Interesting you should ask. Because I had a sales rep from some new bakery here yesterday. What was the name...?"

She was numb. She was so numb, she didn't even feel the ice-water in her veins. "Oh. I understand. So you're going with Lighthouse then?"

Tina snapped her fingers. "Right. Lighthouse, that was the name." She grinned at Rebecca. But Rebecca's utter devastation must have shown on her face because Tina's expression grew concerned. "Hon, we're not going to use them. They came by, but we're sticking with Cookie Nookie. Our customers expect it in our desserts. We aren't going cheap on them now."

Oh, God, I'm going to cry again, she thought in alarm. The numbness had vanished, replaced by a whirlwind of emotions, relief and gratitude chief among them. It was all she could do not to yank Tina out of her chair and hug her for ten minutes straight.

She barely remembered the ride back to Cookie Nookie. She parked in the back and used the back entrance. Her head was crammed full of thoughts and plans and how to survive this Lighthouse Bakery onslaught.

So Jack wanted to play rough, did he? At least Royale was sticking with her. It gave her hope that her other clients would do the same. Or at worst, that they wouldn't drop her entirely, even if they cut back their orders some.

She was confident in her baking, in her product. She knew her cookies would stand up well against Lighthouse's product. Because why would Jack have been so eager to buy (read "steal") her cookie recipe if Lighthouse cookies were superior? Simple, because they weren't.

He could beat her on price, but he couldn't beat her on taste. She could win this. Tomorrow morning she would pay a visit to all her clients and encourage them to stick with her. Hopefully, not too many of them would be drawn to the candle flame of cheapo prices. She simply couldn't afford a price war right now.

She put on her apron and headed for the front door to flip the sign from Closed to Open. But halfway there, she suddenly stopped. The realization hit her hard. She couldn't do this today. She couldn't face the world right now. Too much had gone wrong in the last few days, and it was all looming over her like a huge wave ready to crush her. She'd already cried once this morning, and it wasn't even noon yet. She felt emotionally wrung-out and exhausted. Would it kill her to take a day off? To try and get her head straight?

That settled it. She needed to take a personal day. She quickly scrawled a note and stuck it on the front door.

Sorry to have missed you! Not feeling well today. We'll be open again tomorrow! Thanks for coming by. I appreciate your business!

There. That was true, and hopefully it would mollify any customers who swung by and were disappointed.

She let out a long sigh as she turned everything off and closed up shop. But now her store was so dark and quiet that it was depressing her. It made her worry about going out of business. Taking a day off and closing the store certainly wasn't going to help that any, but she simply didn't have the strength to face people today.

Not after all that had happened.

She got into her car again and drove for her apartment before deciding she didn't want to mope around there either. She decided to just drive and see where she ended up.

Where she finally ended up surprised her.

She was in Portland, down by the waterfront again. She had been drawn here like iron to a magnet. It was a risky move. Liam had his yacht docked here after all. But she would stay far away from that section of the harbor. If she caught sight of his boat on the water, she'd make a quick retreat back to her car.

After parking, she felt like she had made a good choice. This place had memories. Good ones. Today, the sea air was a bit chilly but also bracing. The sky was bright blue and almost cloudless. The sun was so bright that even with the colder wind off the water, she was still comfortable enough.

She bought a coffee and a bagel and found herself a seat on a bench. She watched the ships come and go, watched a lucky fisherman already back with a full haul. She watched the sailboats far out on the horizon where the sunlight glittered on the waves.

The coffee and the sunlight kept her warm, but it was clear that summer was fading fast. New England autumns were beautiful, but she still felt wistful for those warm summer days.

Tomorrow she would have to face the world again. She would have to deal with Jack Meacham and Lighthouse Bakery trying to steal her clients and drive Cookie Nookie into the ground. She was determined to fight him. She wasn't going to go quietly. So what if she had loved his kisses, his touches? What little she had in this world had to be defended.

Rebecca watched the waves, wishing things had turned out differently but not surprised that they hadn't.

She had known, hadn't she? She had feared it. She had told Liam as much.

For once, she wished she'd been wrong.

* * *

Liam

He leaned in close to read the note Rebecca had

stuck to the front door of Cookie Nookie, and his heart sank. "She's not here."

"So she took a personal day," Jack said. "Who can blame her?"

Of course, he couldn't blame her. But it still disturbed him. She was obviously upset. It made him want to rush to her and make things right again. To put a smile back on her face. He didn't know why he couldn't seem to find his inner calm anymore with anything to do with Rebecca, but she had certainly turned his life on its ear.

Perhaps it was simply love. New love that would only get stronger as the days went on. Love that he knew was in danger unless he acted. There was no time to be relaxed, to let the cards fall where they may. *That* was why he couldn't be lackadaisical about this. If he didn't do something, they would lose her.

"We need to find her," he announced to the note on the door.

"You want to interrupt her personal day—"

Liam turned to look at him. Not saying a word.

Jack put up his hands. "You're right. You're right. We'll find her."

Liam nodded, turned on his heel, and marched back to the Benz.

Jack followed him. "I have to admit, I'm a little turned on and a little unsettled by this no-nonsense, man-on-a-mission side of you. It's kind of sexy."

"Yeah, let's just hope Rebecca feels the same way."

"She'll certainly know she's important to you. To *us*. Either that or she'll zap us with a stun gun when we show up uninvited. It could go either way."

Liam snorted and didn't say anything else until they were in the car and the engine was on. "Let's head to her apartment. But first, I want to stop at a flower shop."

"Isn't that a cliché?" Jack asked as they both got inside and he started the engine.

"You're kidding, right? You saw how much she loved those roses we brought her. I'd give her expensive jewelry, but I don't want her to think I'm trying to buy her off. Or trying to impress her. Or that I'm moving too fast."

Jack threw a wry glance his way. "Yeah. I definitely wouldn't want her to think *that*."

"Is that sarcasm, Jack?" Liam asked with deceptive sweetness. "Because it's not helping."

"You're right. Let's go find our girl. After buying some flowers. Ones that have a scent."

Liam raised his eyes toward heaven. "Good lord, the man can actually learn, if you're patient enough."

Jack laughed and pulled into traffic, heading for her place. They were at her apartment complex in less than ten minutes. They made their way up the stairs, and Liam pressed the doorbell.

No one answered.

"I didn't see her car in the lot," Jack said, frowning. "And that car is hard to miss."

Liam nodded, frustration welling inside him. He hadn't seen her car either, but Jack was right. It was hard to miss a car painted like a cookie and with the words *Cookie Nookie* all over it. He knocked anyway, just in case she hadn't heard the doorbell and she had parked on a side-street or something. But in his heart, he knew it was a futile gesture.

Again, no response.

He ran both hands through his hair and let out a long sigh. "Why can't this be easy?"

Jack put a hand on his arm, his expression concerned. "Hey. Don't worry. We'll find her. She can't hide forever." He grinned. "We know where she works. We know where she lives. And we know what she's driving."

"Now we sound like crazy stalkers."

"We're men in love," Jack said with a grin. "There's a difference."

"You're right." He let out another breath, closing his eyes and calming himself down. "But I want to see her again. *Now*. I want to make this right between us." The need was like a crushing pressure on him. The desire to have things right again, to see her and talk with her again weighed on him heavily.

"I know. I feel the same way."

Liam nodded, knowing it was true, despite Jack's jokes or teasing. He could remember the look in Jack's eyes when the three of them had been together, the passion in his touches and in his kisses. He knew without a doubt how the man he loved felt about Rebecca.

"Tell you what," Jack continued. "We both want to see her more than anything. Let's drive around town and see if we can spot her car."

"Then what? Run her off the road? Tail her like undercover cops?"

"No, you moron. We invite her somewhere so we can talk."

He let out a brief laugh. "Even with that unmistakable car, I don't think we're going to find her."

"Hey, I'm more the glass-is-half-empty kind of guy. You should stay positive. This is a small town. If we can't find her today, we'll talk to her tomorrow."

"You're right." He smiled. "Listen to you, so calm and rational. I'm proud."

"It's you rubbing off on me. It means we're perfect for each other. And we both think she's the perfect addition to what we have together."

Liam nodded. Then he grabbed Jack's hand and squeezed it firmly. "Thank you. For being here for me right now."

"I don't want to be anywhere else," Jack said, his eyes grave. "I mean it. We're together on this. I'll do whatever I can to help."

"Then let's go find her. You drive, I'll be the

lookout."

But that was easier said than done. After driving the town twice and even venturing into some of the outlying neighborhoods, they caught no glimpse of Rebecca's distinctive car. They swung by the Cookie Nookie again, but it was still closed. Then they headed back to her apartment. Still no sign of her.

"All right, Jack," he finally admitted during their third drive up the town's main street with no luck. "We're not going to find her today. Do you still want to go sailing?"

Jack looked at him with concern. "Do you? Because right now, we can do anything you want. I know this has been some rough shit."

"I think I need to. Yesterday, it helped calm me. Some time out on the ocean with you is going to save an otherwise wretched and frustrating day."

"Say no more. We're on our way."

Half an hour later, they were driving along the waterfront for the pier where the *Easy Rider* was docked. Liam was listening to the jazz playing on the car's stereo, lost in thoughts of what he would say to Rebecca when he finally found her.

Then he spotted it, bold as day.

He sat bolt upright in his seat and pointed. "Holy shit! That's her car!"

Beside him, Jack glanced where he was pointing and immediately slowed down. "I don't believe it. You're right. She's at the waterfront."

There was no denying that car, not in a thousand years. Not only was the vehicle plastered with the name of her business, but the fake cookie bolted to the top was missing the chocolate kiss. The one that had come flying off after the accident.

He laughed wildly, hope suddenly soaring within him. This had to be some kind of sign. The odds of finding her were so low that this whole scheme had been little more than a wild shot in the dark. But now he couldn't escape the feeling that fate was driving them together. Bringing them together so the three of them could solve this, put it behind them, and get on with the job of falling head over heels in love.

They parked in a nearby pay lot and hurried to Rebecca's car. Liam was nearly running. At first, Jack was trying to look unhurried and unconcerned, but soon he was hustling right alongside Liam. He had to, or Liam would leave him in the dust.

They reached her car and pulled up short. Both of them stood there staring at it. It was empty.

"What should we do now?" Jack asked. "She could be anywhere on the waterfront. If we rush off looking for her, we might miss her. Then she'll drive off again without even knowing we were here."

"You're right. Maybe you should stand guard at her car. I'll go run the waterfront and see if I can find her—"

He cut off abruptly when he suddenly caught sight of her. She was walking along the waterfront, heading in their direction. She hadn't seen them yet because she was looking the other way.

His heart lurched in his chest and began beating twice as fast. He was suddenly all nerves, full of adrenaline, as if he were ready to run the fifty-meter dash.

Jack frowned when Liam stopped talking. He glanced behind him, in the direction Liam was looking. He froze when he saw her.

"I don't even believe it," he said softly. "There she is."

Liam laughed with delight. "It's like a sign from the universe."

"Okay, okay, you New Age lunatic. The universe has made its point. Now, so you want to go to her or let her come to us?"

Liam appreciated that Jack was letting him take the lead on this. Right now, that was what he needed. To take action. "Go to her." He grinned. "Head her off before she can escape in her car."

"God, it sounds as if we're up to something nefarious." But Jack fell right in beside him as Liam hurried down the street.

Rebecca was looking out at the water and walking slowly, her brow knitted, her eyes far away. She was the very picture of a person caught up in their worries or lost in thought. He suspected they were thoughts of him and Jack. He wished she was wearing a smile, but she wasn't.

Then it's your job to put a smile back on her face.

They'd closed within thirty feet of her when she finally spotted them. Her eyes went wide, and she stopped dead. Her mouth opened, but she didn't say a word. She didn't move. Her surprise was so great that

Liam feared it bordered on panic.

"Rebecca," he said as they approached her, desperate to put her at ease. He prayed this wasn't a terrible mistake. From her expression, there was a chance it was. "We need to talk to you. Will you give us a few moments of your time?"

He kept his voice even and calm, even though inside he was shaking like a paint mixer with all his pent-up desire for her, his emotions, his needs, and the simple power of seeing her again. He halted three feet away from her, not touching her, not wanting to get in her personal space until she allowed it. Especially since he wasn't leaving her alone like she'd asked during their morning-after phone conversation.

"How did you find me?" she demanded. Her voice was cold. Her eyes had turned even colder. She didn't move a step closer to them. Her body language was not inviting. Seeing her that way rocked him, even though he'd known this was a risk they'd taken chasing her down.

No, he had to push on with this. If he had jumped out of the plane without a parachute, he'd have to deal with that now. Because he was certain she still felt something for them both. That night they'd spent together, all that passion and those feelings, that couldn't have been a lie. He refused to believe it.

He tried a smile, hoping to thaw her a little, to ease the tension that suddenly crackled in the air. "I love your car, but it will never be anything but impossible to miss." He nodded out toward the water. "My sailboat is moored here. We saw your car, and we had to find you."

Was it him or had her eyes warmed the slightest bit when he said he loved her car? If so, he would take it. Right now, he would take anything.

"All right," she said warily. "I'll accept that. It's my fault. I shouldn't have risked coming down here in the first place." She shrugged and glanced away. "But it has good memories."

Good memories. Hopefully, the time the three of them had spent here still qualified.

"We stopped by your shop and by your apartment," Jack told her gently. "If I were a betting man, I'd say you were trying to avoid us."

She wheeled on him. Her expression going even colder. "*You*? Definitely."

Jack only looked at her, clearly taken aback and not knowing how to reply to the venom in her tone.

Liam didn't know what to say either. Had Jack done something he didn't know about?

"What's that supposed to mean?" Jack finally managed to ask. He still wasn't raising his voice even though he seemed confused and shocked by her cold ferocity.

"You know. Don't play dumb with me."

He shook his head, still looking lost. "You'll have to assume I'm dumb, because I don't know why you're angry. As far as I remember, we all fell asleep together, and I felt like life just might be perfect. But then I woke up and you were gone. So much for perfect."

She glared at him, her teeth clenched. There were two bright spots of color high on her cheeks. She was furious, and she was hurt. Her eyes, as angry as they were, had also filled with tears. She was fighting them, but Liam could tell she was ripped up inside. That made him ache to comfort her in any way he could.

But that was the problem. He *couldn't*. Not until

he found out what was wrong between them. Right now, he felt their last hope of love with Rebecca slipping away fast. Sliding right through his fingers, even as he held on for dear life.

"We *don't* know, Rebecca," he said softly. "That's why we had to find you. To talk with you. Please. Tell us."

A tear slipped from one eye and ran down her cheek. She wiped it away with the back of her hand, the motion jerky and angry. "I told you over the phone this wouldn't work. Then you had to go and prove me right. You couldn't even wait a day. A *day!*"

He was lost. He had no idea what she was talking about. Was she angry because they'd come looking for her? Did she expect them to simply walk away as if their time together had meant nothing?

"Whatever it is," he said, "we can work it out. But right now, we're only confused. Are you upset because we came to see you here? Maybe that was over the line, but—"

"*No.* I'm angry because this morning I found out what I suspected all along. All my fears were proved true." She glared daggers at Jack. "Because of you. You and your...unfettered greed!"

Jack still looked mystified...and a bit offended. "I need more to go on than that, Rebecca."

"Of course you do," she snarled. "You probably destroy businesses left, right, and sideways, and you can't keep track of them all." She leaned toward him, her pretty eyes narrowed. "But my business means everything to me. So you messed with the wrong girl this time, buddy."

"There's been some kind of mistake," Liam said, unable to quiet the alarm bells ringing in his head. "Jack doesn't destroy businesses. And he certainly doesn't want to destroy yours."

Now she turned that fiery, hurt, and angry look on him. "Oh, is that right? Maybe you don't know him as well as you thought."

He frowned. "You need to explain yourself. I think you owe us that much."

"Fine. I'll spell it out for you. This morning I lost one of my best customers. The owner is going to buy the cookies for their cookie dessert from Lighthouse Bakery starting next month because *you* sent a sales rep there to undercut me completely." She was blinking back tears, her voice shaking because she was so mad. "As if that wasn't enough, then you sent someone to try and take my other big restaurant client with the same shady tactics." She put her hands on her hips and glared at Jack. "But that one didn't work, did it? They're going to stick with me, so ha!"

Liam's heart was thudding in his chest like a drum in a funeral dirge. What the hell was this? He turned slowly to look at Jack. "Is that true?"

Jack had gone pale, his expression absolutely stricken. Seeing that, Liam's heart went into freefall. Something had gone very, very wrong.

"I got a call earlier," Jack said. "Yesterday, I think. It was my sales manager, Susie Ford. I was barely paying attention because I was worried." He paused, closing his eyes and tipping his head back. The grimace on his face spoke volumes. "I was worried about you and me, Liam. Just as much as I was worried about Rebecca."

Rebecca was watching him closely, her expression screaming that she wasn't impressed with his story.

Liam would give him the benefit of the doubt, as

he always would for the rest of his life. He loved the man. It was the least he could do. But he needed to know the truth. "What happened?"

"I guess Susie was more enthusiastic than I expected. She told me she had secured a bunch of restaurant clients from Portland and other places...and at least one from Fremont. At the time, I didn't even make the connection." He met Rebecca's scrutinizing gaze. "Her job is to find us new markets and opportunities, but I swear I didn't send her out to steal business from you. That was never my intention."

"It doesn't matter if you intended that or not," Rebecca said. "Because that's exactly what happened. This isn't some cute little hobby of mine, Jack. This is how I feed myself and keep the lights on. You might not have to worry about any of that anymore with all your money and your fancy house and car, but I sure do."

There were tears glistening on her cheeks. She stopped and scrubbed at them angrily.

Liam had already come to know that she didn't like crying, especially not in front of other people. It was proof of how deeply upset she was that she couldn't hold those tears in check.

Rebecca suddenly stepped around them, heading for her car.

Jack caught her arm. "Rebecca, please. Let me explain—"

"What exactly is there to explain, you greedy jerk? You got your rocks off, the two of you, fucking the poor girl with the silly car who's a sucker for people who like her cookies—"

"Stop it!" Liam snapped at her. He'd had all he could take of this scene. "Enough of that kind of talk, Rebecca."

She blinked at him and stopped, her mouth open, her eyes wide.

Good. He had her damn attention.

Now that he did, he reached out and touched her cheek tenderly. It was a risk, touching her with all these negative emotions flying around. He wouldn't have been surprised if she had knocked his hand away or drew back out of his reach.

But she didn't. She stayed still. She allowed his touch.

No, *more* than that. As he cupped her cheek, he

felt her lean into his hand as if aching for the touch. That was enough. That gave him what he needed. It was the sign that told him that even now, they could fix this. All this hurt and misunderstandings could be set straight.

But he had to do this right. There was no room for mistakes, no margin for error.

"It hurts me when you talk that way about yourself," he told her, looking straight into her big eyes. "Because it's not true. The time we shared together is something I'll never forget. You called Jack greedy, but it's me who's greedy. Because I want you. And I want him. Now that I've tasted you, now that I've had you in my life, I can't be happy without you."

"The same goes for me," Jack said, very softly, very un-Jack like. But it was powerful nonetheless because of the way he was looking at her with so much need and passion and love that it took Liam's breath away. "I'm so sorry about what happened between us, but I would never knowingly hurt you. I'll make this right. I promise."

The way Jack was looking at Rebecca seemed to have the same effect on her as it had on Liam—stealing her breath and her words away—because she didn't make a sound. The anger left her face. She looked stunned…and a little hopeful.

Liam seized on that hope. It was the best chance they'd had.

Jack had managed to disarm her anger—at least for the time being. Now it was Liam's chance to talk, to convince her, and he knew he didn't have much time to make this right.

"You are so kind, funny, and beautiful that I know without a doubt that I need you in my life," Liam said. "We came looking for you, needing to make that absolutely clear. Whatever happened with one of Jack's employees and your customer, I promise that we'll make it right. But you need to give us a chance. You need to stop tearing yourself down, or talking as if what we shared together was nothing more than a one-night stand and we're going to vanish into the sunset." He leaned toward her, every word vibrating with feeling. "It *was* one night, but it was the first of a great many unforgettable nights to come. Or it will be if you'll stop running, take a chance, and trust us."

She closed her eyes, more tears running down

her cheeks. He ever-so-gently wiped some of them away. They were warm and wet on his skin. It hurt his heart to see her this upset. He only wanted her happy. Just like he wanted Jack happy. Usually, he could do it. He was easygoing, made people laugh and smile, made them feel good. But all the cards were on the table, and he knew without a doubt, from somewhere deep within himself, that she belonged with them. That the two of them could make her happy if she would only give them a chance.

"I've been doing things on my own for so long," she said quietly, her eyes still closed. "I don't know if I can trust. When I lost that customer...I panicked."

Jack moved to her side and gently but firmly pulled her into a hug. Liam saw her tense and almost resist for a fraction of a second before giving in. She pressed her face against Jack's chest, sobbing quietly.

Jack kissed the top of her head, a gesture of infinite tenderness. "Sweetheart, I understand completely. You may not believe me, but I was in your shoes once, a long time ago. I'm sorry I wasn't watching my people more closely, especially after making you promises. That's on me. Can you forgive me? Will you give me the chance to make this right?"

She looked up at him with her big brown eyes. Slowly, she nodded.

Jack's smile could have lit the world during a solar eclipse. He closed his eyes, leaning his head back with unmistakable relief. "Thank you. I know we got off to a rocky start. I know I'm not the easiest guy to get along with. Just ask Liam, he can tell you."

"He's an ass," Liam said, feeling elated that they had gotten this far.

Rebecca laughed, wiping her eyes again. "You're right. But so was I. I shouldn't have run out on you both. I just wanted...not to be the one ditched. I didn't want to see any regret or second thoughts in your eyes. I thought it would hurt less if I was the one to end it."

"Why would you think we would want to hurt you, beautiful?" Liam asked, a note of astonishment in his voice.

She shook her head. "Because it was too good to be true. Because it was moving so fast, and I knew I had already lost my heart to you both. It was too fast, too dangerous, and I was sure I would be hurt. So I tried..."

"You tried to protect yourself," Jack finished for her. "I get it. I do. But sometimes life gives you something great."

Liam was smiling at her fondly. "And sometimes you only need to sit back, believe you deserve it, and let the good things happen." He slid his arms around her. Jack saw what he intended and gently withdrew so Liam could pull Rebecca fully into his embrace.

Liam kissed her, pulling her even closer, loving the sensation of her lush body pressed against his. He could feel her heart beating fast. As fast as his heart was beating. He deepened the kiss, pouring all his passion into it.

His heart was slamming in his chest, and he was short of breath when he finally withdrew his lips from hers. She looked just as shaken up, her eyes wide, and her lips swollen. He could kiss those lips forever and never tire of them. Or of her.

"I'm choosing to believe," Rebecca said solemnly, but a hint of a smile lingered on those kiss-swollen lips.

"Good," Liam said firmly. "Besides, you don't

have anything to worry about. Your cookies are better than Lighthouse's cookies. I should know. I'm an expert."

"Hey!" Jack protested as Rebecca broke out in laughter.

Passing people glanced their way, but Liam ignored them all. What did he care what people thought of them or their unique relationship? He was doing something good in the world. He was making a man he cared for and a woman he cared for as happy as he could make them.

That was something to be proud of.

Jack winked at him and turned to Rebecca. "Tomorrow morning, I'll make the thing with Susie right."

She tilted her head and looked at him boldly. "No. Don't. If that owner is going to be cheap and turn his back on me after all these years, then let him. Like Liam said, my cookies are better. I bet he comes crawling back in three months, begging to use my cookies again after his customers start complaining."

"That's the spirit!" Jack said, grinning from ear to ear.

Now it was Jack's turn to pull her in for a passionate kiss instead of the tender ones he'd given her before. It was a memory he would cherish, seeing them together like this after a storm that had threatened to drive them apart forever. He hoped for many, many more memories as precious as this one.

And he was positive that the universe would give new, cherished memories to him, as long as he did his part to make sure both his special people were loved and cherished.

"So do you want this?" Jack asked Rebecca after the kiss, holding her gaze with an intensity that revealed how important her answer would be to him. "Because I want this. The three of us. Together. Nothing could make me happier."

"I do," she whispered. "I was afraid it was too good to be true. I was afraid to open up my heart to being happy. But now I think I only cut off my nose to spite my face. So...if you'll forgive me for vanishing on you..." She swallowed and gave them the sweetest smile in the world. "Then maybe you'll let me make it up to you? I have a few things in mind you might like."

Liam groaned, those big eyes and full lips of

hers driving him to distraction. What she was implying already had his cock getting hard. He wanted her so badly. He wanted her and Jack naked and in bed, wrapped in silk sheets, with sex and sweat in the air. God, he was going to drive both of them wild when he got them alone again. It was a vow.

"You don't need to make anything up to me," he finally managed to say to her. "But if you're thinking what I'm thinking—and it's naughty as hell—then I'm so damn eager to let you try that I'm standing here on the waterfront with a raging hard-on."

That made Jack and Rebecca laugh. He loved the sound of her laughter. And he loved how Jack's eyes warmed when he laughed. The two of them laughing together was music to his ears.

"Now," Liam continued. "What do you say to some sailing?" He glanced at the sky, which was perfectly cloudless, and he felt the wind, which would be more than enough to fill his sails. "I have plenty of food and spirits on board. I'll cook us up a meal. We can eat on deck, watch the sun go down and watch the stars come out." He let a wicked smile take his face. "Then Jack and I can show you exactly how much you mean to us."

Jack nodded, caught up in his enthusiasm. "We'll show you until you can't take any more. That's another promise. One you can put in the bank, my little cookie queen."

Rebecca's cheeks were flushed, but he knew it was desire, not embarrassment or uncertainty. Her eyes told him the only story he needed to know. She was all-in.

But she surprised them both with a kiss, one for each of them. She stood between them and linked arms with them. "All right, mateys! Escort me to your scurvy galleon!"

Liam rubbed his chin with his free hand, looking thoughtful. "I'm not sure a galleon can have scurvy."

She stuck out her tongue at him. "Don't give me your lip, ye big-cocked scallywag. I expect to be taken aboard and ravished at every opportunity."

Jack was grinning and shaking his head. "You are one of a kind. And I love it." He stepped back and swept into an elegant bow. "My lady, your wish is our command."

Together, they walked to his sailboat. They spent

the night on the water, anchored beneath the stars on a calm sea. They made love, and they made memories. The happiness and love between them would only grow deeper, day by day, through rough seas or calm seas.

Because they had each other.

EPILOGUE

Rebecca

One year later...

"This is a macaroon," Rebecca said, handing a sample to a little girl about six years old and then giving one to her mother. "The ingredients are all-natural. All our cookies are baked fresh, with minimal preservatives."

The girl had big brown eyes. She scarfed the cookie down and wiped away the crumbs with the back of her hand. "That was good. Mommy, can I have another?"

The girl's mother took a bite of her macaroon. Her eyebrows shot up. "That *is* good! We'll definitely take a box." She paused and took another bite. "Make that two. Can we order these online?"

"Yes, you can," Rebecca said with a smile. She got the boxes of cookies and pointed to the outside packaging with her logo on it. "This has the Cookie Nookie website address on it. We offer free shipping on large orders."

As the woman dug through her pocketbook, Rebecca spotted Jack and Liam across the aisle at the bustling Lighthouse Bakery booth. Jack was wearing jeans and a work shirt as he chatted with one of his marketing people who had done much of this year's booth design. He saw her looking his way, smiled, and waved.

Liam, on the other hand, wasn't wearing a suit this time at the tradeshow. He was wearing khakis and a short-sleeved button-down, unbuttoned of course, over a bright red T-shirt. Liam sauntered over from the big Lighthouse booth. She loved the way he moved. Languid. Graceful. With the smoothness of a wave rolling up a beach in a gentle surf. But there was nothing languid in his gaze. It was as hot as the summer sun.

She turned her attention back to her customer, but she felt her skin getting hot anyway. The way her two men looked at her got her all riled up and heated. Right now, both of them looked as if they wanted to leave the tradeshow early to drag her home and get up to all kinds of sexy mischief.

She really liked how they thought.

"Mom, what's a 'nookie?'" the little girl asked, tugging on her mother's sleeve.

Rebecca leaned down so she was looking the girl in the eye. She gave her warmest smile. "It's a play on the word 'nook.' My store is tiny. Nook means like a little corner or recess. Somewhere a little secluded. See?"

The girl looked dubious but nodded anyway.

"I'm going to have to tell my friends about these," the mother said, handing over a debit card. "This is *really* good."

"Thank you," Rebecca replied, using the card reader on her smartphone, emailing a receipt, then waving as the mother and daughter moved off with their boxes of cookies.

Every sale today made her feel good. The crowd this year was heavier than last year. Lighthouse Bakery Company was throwing a big vacation getaway sweepstakes. It had brought out a curious crowd... A crowd that really wanted a free vacation. But lots of them liked free cookie samples too. So she'd been very busy since the doors had opened. And she'd been soaking up the compliments. People were surprised by how good her cookies tasted, and they usually wanted to buy a box. Or two.

Liam didn't say a word as he reached her booth. He simply came over, walked behind the table, and swept her into a kiss. It wasn't a G-rated kiss either. She let him have his way, enjoying every minute of it, not caring a bit if they were getting stares.

When he finally let her go, she struggled to catch her breath again. She made a show of fixing her hair and rearranging her rumpled dress. Then she scowled at him, although judging by his self-satisfied grin, he knew she wasn't mad.

"Public displays of affection are frowned upon at tradeshows, you know," she said primly. "At least for the food industry."

"They can arrest me," Liam said. "I'll tell the judge it was worth it as he throws away the key."

She laughed. "It will be hard to take our Caribbean vacation with you in the slammer."

"Send me a picture of you. Make it poster-sized. I'll use it to hide the hole I'll painstakingly dig through the wall to escape back to you." He grinned and shrugged. "Or I'll post bail. Whatever works."

He put his arm around her. She snuggled against him. There was nothing like the feeling of being held by her two men. Simultaneously comforting and exciting. She never got tired of it.

He looked down at her, giving her that warm, charming smile that melted her like a chocolate chip in a fresh-baked cookie. "I overheard you talking to that little girl." His grin widened, grew mischievous. "You're still claiming 'nookie' means 'nook.' I guess if you say it enough, someone will start to believe you."

"Hush," she scolded. "What fun is a playful double entendre if you spend all your time pointing it out?"

"I'm still shocked the old biddies and crusty old men on the city council let you use that name. Especially Mr. Grumpy Cat Face." Liam rubbed his jawline, shaking his head a little. "Wonders never cease."

"I'm not going to tell them what it *could* mean." She narrowed her eyes at him. "And neither are you."

He made a show of zipping his lips, then locking them and tossing the key. Which was so silly that she giggled again.

Jack finished talking to his employee and made a beeline for them. Jack's walk was completely different from Liam's. He always walked as if he was charging ahead. Or late to be somewhere. He looked as if he would crash his way through a wall if a wall got in his way. But even though he moved like that, he still was polite, waiting patiently as a family with a stroller crossed down the aisle in front of him.

But when Jack finally reached her, he drew her into his arms and kissed her soundly. Then he broke off long enough to kiss his way up her neck as she giggled and her nipples tightened with a sudden surge of desire.

"PDA," she managed to gasp. "We'll cause a scandal in the baking industry!"

"Good thing they won't be around to see what we do on the deck of Liam's boat," Jack murmured against her skin, sending a delightful shiver through her body. "Because that's going to be hot and nasty."

"Oooh. I like the sound of that," she whispered.

"And as for scandals..." Jack leaned over, grabbed Liam, and pulled him into a kiss too.

She watched them, marveling at how hot they looked together, and how much it turned her on. That was another thing she never got tired of.

"Would you look at that, Bethie?" an old woman said cheerily. "It makes me glad we came today."

Blushing, Rebecca turned toward the voice. Two short, old ladies with huge, gaudy handbags were watching the three of them. She half-expected them to be outraged, but they pleasantly surprised her because they were both smiling.

Bethie patted her friend's arm. "Come on now, Carol, it's rude to stare at the young people in love. We'll come back for cookies later."

Laughing together, the two old ladies kept walking down the aisle.

"Look at that," Jack said from beside her. "We didn't get thrown out."

"Not yet anyway," Liam happily added. "There's still time."

She shook her head. They were incorrigible, but she loved it.

"How's business?" Jack asked her. "Every time I look over here, you have more customers. I'm getting jealous."

"I've been super busy," she teased. "How's business on your side of the aisle? Am I stealing all your customers?"

"Lots of people want to win a free vacation," Jack said. He shrugged. "But since we're going for brand recognition in local stores, it all works out in the end. Meanwhile, it looks like my Cookie Girl Genius is finally getting some of the recognition she so richly deserves."

"For the record, that is *not* my new nickname. But I've actually sold forty-five boxes of cookies. Look, I'm almost out!"

Liam leaned in and kissed her on the neck, then nuzzled her ear. She practically purred. Someone was certainly horny today. It thrilled her that she could still rile them up like this. Both of them always made her feel beautiful and wanted. As if she meant the world to them.

Because they certainly meant the world to her.

"I would say I'm impressed by those numbers," Jack told her, "but your cookies are divine, so you selling all of them is no surprise. I *am* surprised that they don't rename this trade show *The Grand Cookie Nookie Festival* and have done with it."

She laughed, feeling warm inside at the praise. So much had changed since last year's tradeshow. It boggled the mind whenever she paused to think about it.

First, she had two wonderful, amazing men in her life. Did she forget to mention how gorgeous they were? It was hard not to drool over them sometimes. Maybe that wasn't ladylike, but she liked to indulge in a little ogling from time to time. What girl didn't need some hot man-candy in her life? She happened to be blessed with not one but two hot-as-hell man-candy samples. Why pretend to be demure about it?

Although, sometimes she was afraid she was *too* lucky. Sometimes she woke up at three in the morning, her heart pounding, terrified this had all been a dream. A wonderful, magical dream but a dream nonetheless.

But Liam and Jack's warm, naked bodies lying right next to hers put such fears to rest.

The second huge change was that she was rich. She was one million, one-hundred thousand dollars rich to be exact. Well, before taxes. The government would take a big bite out of that haul.

It wasn't money from Liam or Jack—not directly anyway, as if they were her sugar daddies. Yes, they lavished gifts on her because they were generous, and Jack especially liked to show how he felt with gifts to her and to Liam.

But this was money from Lighthouse Bakery Company to buy the rights to three of her "famous" cookie recipes for a big push Lighthouse was making into snacks and desserts. She was paid a huge chunk of money and would still be able to use her own recipes for her shop for as long as she wanted. Jack had explained he was eager to bring her cookies—which Liam loved almost as much as sex and sailing—to the rest of the country.

"This is win-win," Jack had told her months ago, lying naked on the bed with his hands behind his head after one very energetic round of sex between the three of them. "The country gets delicious, as-healthy-as-cookies-can-be cookies, Lighthouse makes tons of profit, and you get set up for life. You won't need us. You won't need anybody."

She had glared at him. "I'll still need you. Both of you. You're not getting off that easy."

Liam had loved that. He had claimed her mouth with a fierce kiss, and then they had proceeded to make love to her again, leaving her exhausted and utterly sated.

But the truth was, she hadn't agreed to sell at first. She could use the money, sure, but she worried she was being greedy. Or that this was a handout she hadn't earned. What if her cookies failed and

Lighthouse went out of business? Everyone would hate her. Would Jack blame her? Why would she risk that?

Liam had been the one to finally convince her. Liam seemed to understand her perspective. He didn't pressure her, but he did, gently, discuss it with her at length while sunbathing on the deck of his sailboat. He reassured her that this deal would never come between them, even if it failed. Jack wasn't like that. And this deal was about her and what she'd achieved with her talents. She needed to stop doubting herself and accept what she was worth. She was priceless to them, but this deal would set her up on her own merits for the rest of her life, no matter what.

She liked that. She liked the security of it, the same way she liked owning her own little store and talking with the customers. She was already thinking about hiring some people to take over for her...so she wouldn't have to get up at the crack of dawn to start baking, and maybe a bookkeeper to keep the book headache straight.

So she had accepted. But she wasn't interested in their money. She was interested in their love. Love they never seemed to run out of.

Things hadn't been completely smooth. Even though Jack owned the company, the deal had to go through approval with the board of directors, who were skeptical of either the value or the price. Luckily for her, a few cookie samples of the recipes they were buying had been enough to convince them to sign off on it.

She was staggered to think that much money actually belonged to her...right now sitting in the bank because she wasn't sure what to do with it all yet. Even after paying off every business loan and the loan on the Cookie Nookie mobile, she still had tons. And even after she had signed up to support every single charity she saw on TV for abused pets and feeding people in other countries, that still left her a huge amount of money.

As much as she loved the security of all of that money—and being able to pay for healthcare and retirement, keeping her shop open and putting food on the table for the rest of her life—she knew the greatest treasure wasn't the payout. It was the two amazing men she loved. Liam and Jack. The three of them fit together perfectly in every way that mattered. When they showed her how much they loved her, she felt like the luckiest woman in the universe.

"What are you thinking about, beautiful?" Liam asked, gazing into her eyes. He had that lazy smile on his lips, but his gaze was warm and loving. He was one of the most caring men she'd ever met.

"How rich I am," she said, and that made Jack burst out laughing.

Liam grinned, shaking his head. "Jack has turned you into a monster. Next, you'll be buying a huge yacht shaped like a cookie and setting off to sail the world."

"Hey!" She punched him on the arm. It hurt her knuckles more than it hurt Liam. The man had shoulder muscles as hard as a steel door. "Is that a knock on my cookie-painted car with the giant cookie on top? You may be making fun now, but I'll show you. I'll have the fanciest snack-shaped boat in the world!"

"Careful, Liam," Jack warned. "I think she's serious. You might face some real competition on the water."

She mock-glared at Jack too. "What I *meant*—well, mostly—was how rich I was to have both of you in my life."

Jack leaned in and stole another kiss. She could tell that her words had touched him. "That goes double for us, Rebecca."

Liam nodded and embraced her from behind, holding her tightly, his hug a comfort as it always was. "Even if we lost everything tomorrow," he said softly, "I would still think myself filthy rich if I had you and Jack in my life."

Jack grinned and gave him a scorching kiss. Then he kissed her again. This time they didn't have an audience of old ladies. Or maybe they did. She had stopped paying attention to anyone around her except for her two guys.

"After this is over," Jack said, "I can't wait to get out on the water, just the three of us, sailing our way to bright sun and warm beaches." He gave her, then Liam, a look hot with desire. "And nude sunbathing on our deck."

Liam grinned. "I thought we were going to spend all our time below deck fucking like rabbits?"

"That too," Jack agreed.

"Guys, guys," she interrupted. "Someone's going to have to actually steer the ship."

"Good point." Jack glanced at Liam with a serious expression. "We'll have to fuck like rabbits above deck while you man the helm."

Liam shook his head, amused. "You two are something else. We'll drop sails and drop anchor before dropping boxers and panties. That's a rule."

She giggled because it sounded so silly...even though that was probably a good rule to have.

"Aye, aye, captain!" she said, saluting. "But until then, are you interested in helping a local shop and community favorite hand out samples and do our part to fill the world with cookies?"

"Challenge accepted," Jack said. "Liam, don't eat all the samples. They're for the customers."

"Resisting temptation isn't going to be easy."

God, she loved them so much. "Be good for now, and I promise to make it up to both of you later."

"Now, I do love the sound of that," Liam said.

The three of them stood together as more people entered the tradeshow. She stood between them. Jack's arm was around her shoulders. Liam's arm was around her waist. She thought her heart might just burst with happiness. It had been an amazing, life-changing year. She was eager to see what the future would bring.

But whatever might come, she was eager to face it with Liam and Jack, two men she loved, and the two men who loved her. And that was even better than all the cookies in the world.

~ ABOUT THE AUTHOR ~

Cari loves all kinds of romance, but right now she's hooked on menage romances. She sews and she snowboards and she likes hot chocolate afterwards. Her dog is named after her first cat, go figure. *Catering to Billionaires* was her first book, followed by *Triple Layer Love, A Spirited Threesome, Too Hot to Handle, Finding Their Treasure, Serving All Three, Cookie Nookie, Wild Ride,* and *Fortune's Fancy.*

Look for more of Cari Griffin's romances coming soon.

~ AVAILABLE NOW FROM ETOPIA PRESS ~

Serving All Three
Cari Griffin

When a European prince and his valet lover meet an American artist, none of them are prepared for their scorching-hot menage or the scandal it creates...

Nicolaus Laurenz thought he had an easy life as the prince of a small and wealthy European country. He's one of most eligible bachelors in Europe, but rumors about his love affair with his valet, Kyle Dumont, have stirred controversy. People want him to marry and produce an heir. Even though he and Kyle have indulged in the occasional threesome, he doesn't believe there's a woman that exists who will be perfect for them both. Until he meets Charlotte North. The curvy and cute glass artist from Detroit instantly catches his attention. Nicolaus has always been a black sheep, but when he sees his valet is just as attracted to Charlotte as he is, he knows this is his chance. They might have finally found a woman perfect to share their love with...

Charlotte North thought she was living her dream life, studying glass blowing in Europe with a famous master. Until she stumbles across the gorgeous prince and his hot manservant as she's delivering a glass sculpture to the palace. She is helpless to resist their charms, and the night she spends with them leaves her breathless and yearning for more. The romance is a whirlwind, and she's loving every minute of her secret tryst with two men who make her heart melt. But secrets can't be kept for long among the royal family. When rumors reach the tabloids, the scandal and publicity threaten to drive them apart for good. Love requires sacrifice, but how much is too much, and can their new love endure the storm?

Wild Ride

Cari Griffin

A billionaire and his polo player lover will take this curvy girl on the ride of her life...

Sara Phillips is caught in the date from Hell at a fancy, five-star country club. Sure, she's a curvy woman, but there's no excuse for the body shaming from her blind date. When things go even worse from there, two gorgeous men intervene to set things right. And they set it right in oh so many ways. Both Malcolm and Alex are sexy, charming men who share a love of polo and each other. But after a night of unforgettable passion, Sara walks away. She's a simple florist, after all. She doesn't belong in their glamorous, high-society world.

Alex Hobbs loves two things. Polo and Malcolm. But things have been tense between the two of them lately. Both men are bisexual, but Malcolm wants a woman in his life too and won't settle down with only another man. After their perfect night with Sara, Alex believes their problems are solved. Their menage is hot enough to blister paint, and surely they've found a wonderful woman to share their love and success. But then Sara leaves, and Malcolm might be the one responsible for driving her away before they have the chance to turn passion into lasting love...

Malcolm Kendrick built a billionaire fortune with a huge craft store chain. He's been friends and lovers with Alex for a long time. Still, he's not willing to settle on one side of the spectrum because he loves women too. At first, Sara seems like the perfect solution for them both. She's kind, sexy, and willing to let herself go wild. But his chain stores have put the little floral shop where she works in danger. How can the three of them have any hope of staying together if he's costing her everything?

Made in the USA
Middletown, DE
09 April 2020